MW00910553

THE VAMPIRE RELATIONSHIP GUIDE, VOLUME 1: MEETING AND MATING

Evelyn Lafont

Erin —

Thanks for entering! Hope you enjoy the book!

Evelyn Lafont

The Vampire Relationship Guide, Volume 1: Meeting and Mating. Copyright © 2011 Evelyn Lafont. All rights reserved worldwide. Text cannot be distributed without prior written permission of the author, with the exception of brief, attributed quotations on web and print media. For questions or permission of usage, please email EvelynLafont@Yahoo.com.

This is a work of fiction. Any resemblance herein to real people or places is purely coincidental.

To Hubby.

TABLE OF CONTENTS

ACKNOWLEDGMENTS

A book is, I now know, not a solitary endeavor. Thanks to the editing team at BubbleCow for steering my prose in the right direction, 52Novels for help with the layout, Hubby for the amazing cover, and Christine LePorte for her fine-toothed comb proofreading method and her ability to pay way more attention to the amount of time between days than I can.

I'd like to give a special thanks to my beta readers Hayley, Shannon, Jane, and Jenn M. Some of you got this in Frankenstein format and were still able to give me great feedback on story and pace.

Finally, a special thanks to Des, who doesn't even read fiction but still noticed that my penchant for starting sentences with the word "So" was super annoying.

THE VAMPIRE RELATIONSHIP GUIDE, VOLUME 1: MEETING AND MATING

PART 1 – HOW TO MEET A VAMPIRE

Vampires are a hot commodity on the dating scene. Generally considered attractive, their powerful eyes, super-human strength, incredible longevity and skills in the bedroom are world-renowned. But like the elusive creatures of the night they show in movies, a single vampire is hard to find unless you know where to look.

The very best place to meet a vampire is at a social event, like a party. Parties offer the chance to…

—Excerpt from *VampLure Magazine*

CHAPTER 1

Have you ever had an inexplicable attraction to a certain type of person? Maybe you fawn over brunets, or men over six feet tall make your knees weak. For me, it's vampires. Just knowing that someone is a little long in the eyetooth and favors a neck bite over a brownie bite reduces me to a blubbering puddle of drool.

Why vampires? Well, let's be real here; they are all—each and every one—extremely hot. Modern books and movies get the idea right. Vampires have perfect, glowy complexions; they don't get dark circles under their eyes; they don't have to deal with dandruff or canker sores; vampires never get bloated, wrinkled, saggy, or pimpled. Not to mention the fact that vampires take creating other fangsters seriously. Who would you pick to turn into the undead so they'd live forever among your kind, your average looking run-of-the-mill human—or the exceptionally beautiful?

Unfortunately, by the time I reached my thirty-second birthday I had yet to meet a single, *datable* male vampire. Since I work in a bridal shop the unmarried male vampires that I'd met were all about to head down the aisle and weren't available for sexy fun time with me. And since vampires marry often enough to make it a little less special each time and have weddings only to appease their human fiancée's family, they didn't exactly bring along single, fang-bearing groomsmen.

I was lamenting my bad fortune while working one night when Craig–a married vampire, friend, and mailman–stopped in to deliver the evening's mail. I heard the tinkle of the bell above the bridal shop door just as I finished hanging up a pink tulle nightmare of a dress that a delusional middle-aged bride had tried on. Oh, she wasn't delusional because she was middle-aged and getting married, she was delusional because pink tulle wouldn't look good on Gwyneth Paltrow, much less on a five-foot three-inch overweight woman with a ruddy complexion.

I put on my *Hello, yes-I am Josie, your sophisticated bridal shop employee* smile-sneer only to find Craig carrying his mail sack and staring intently as he separated out the mail that was for us and that was for our neighbor, Little Tony's Pizzeria.

"Hey, Craig. How's it going tonight?" Craig and I had an almost identical conversation every night. I liked talking to Craig; he was about five feet ten inches tall, with short blond hair and a perpetual five o'clock shadow, solidly built and easygoing. In life, he had been a farmer and he never really lost that average-guy approachability.

"S'okay, Josie. How's the bridal biz?" I knew Craig didn't actually care about how business was. He also didn't care a thing about weddings in general. Craig had been married for thirty years to his wife, Sandra. She was his fifty-second bride, which shows that even a vampire can be of the marrying kind.

"Same as always. Well, except that it's my birthday today, yet here I am working. Happy birthday to me?"

"Oh man, no, your birthday? I didn't get you anything. Oh, but hey-I got something you can do tomorrow. We'll call it a birthday present from me to you."

"Why? What's so special about tomorrow night?"

"You haven't heard? Gregory Bullster is in town. He's an old friend of mine, going back five centuries. He's throwing a big bash over in his new condo on Beach Drive. I can't go, I gotta work. Why don't you take my invitation?"

Gregory Bullster was on Forbes' list of richest vampires. He was famous, hot (well, I didn't actually know what he looked like but anecdotal evidence abounded), and super successful. Naturally, I was intrigued, thrilled, and about to pee all over the tacky blue carpet of the shop from excitement. "Craig, that would be awesome!"

"Well, sure, I'm glad I was on the route tonight." He added with a slight smile, "I bet there'll be a lot of single guys there-hell, even Gregory is single."

The time I spent at the shop had taught me exactly how to meet single vampires. Through many conversations with successful brides-to-be I had it on good authority that parties were the best place to meet hot vampire bachelors. Unfortunately, I'm not really fashionable enough to be in the know about these kinds of events. Vampires generally live extremely long lives while simultaneously amassing a great deal of wealth, and the wealthy and beautiful are a bit (okay, a whole lot) out of my league.

This meant that Craig was giving me the golden ticket into a vampire hot guy factory that I might never have the chance to enter again. My eyes were starting to glaze over at the thought of it. I imagined myself as a thinner, more feminine Augustus Glut trying to lick all the vampire hotties and eventually falling into a moving stream of them.

Craig rooted around in his mail bag past the Sears catalogs and bills from Florida Power and pulled out an envelope with a ragged flap. It was cream colored and thick, textured, and lined with gold foil. He handed it to me and I took it on my palms like it was as delicate as the Dead Sea Scrolls.

I fingered the light texturing on the surface and rubbed my thumb on the cool, smooth foil inside.

"Craig, this is the most wonderful thing anyone has ever done for me." I breathed the words as if speaking them in louder tones would ruin the moment.

Craig laughed. "Josie, you know that's just the envelope, right? You haven't even looked at the invitation yet."

I screamed and slowly ran my fingers into the envelope and felt the hard edge of an invitation card. I eased it out, wanting the excitement to last as long as possible.

Eventually I had the entire card removed and I closed my eyes to steady myself before taking a peek. I looked down and found a simple card in that same ivory color with gold script text announcing the party of Mr. Gregory Bullster. Tomorrow night, 8 PM. I shivered with anticipation.

I don't really know how long I stood there slowly tugging the card out of the envelope, molesting it with my eyeballs, then slowly easing it back into the folded paper container, but when I glanced up Craig was staring at me and looked like he needed a cold shower. I blushed and turned away.

"Well, I, uh, guess I gave the invitation to the right girl. When you go make sure you tell Gregory that I sent my regards."

Now Craig had done it. He had charged me with a task that meant I couldn't spend my night standing against the wall like an observer. Instead, I simply had to talk to Mr. Rich and Single Vampire Guy.

But first, I had to figure out what to wear.

CHAPTER 2

"Why in the world are you calling me to ask what to wear to a vampire party? I'm married. With children. Really young, gooey and greasy toddler type children. The last time I left the house in the middle of the night it was to get Children's Nyquil to drug my...err, to comfort my sick child so that he could sleep. What do I know from vampire party attire?"

When faced with indecision about what to wear to what could shape up to be the most important party I'd ever gone to, naturally I'd called my best friend, Alena. In college, Alena had been a real party animal. Of course, she wasn't anymore, but since I spent my college years working three jobs and trying to support my broke ass, I didn't get the chance to party like other people my age so I thought she might have a better idea of what to wear than I would.

I was sitting on the floor in the bedroom area of my one-room cottage. I was cross-legged in nothing but my underwear and bra. I had several dresses lying out on my bed but hadn't made a real decision past my matching set of black undies, which were acquiring an alarming amount of lint as I sat on the floor. There were two dresses that I had pretty much narrowed it down to. "Alena, I just need some feed-back, 'kay? Short and sparkly, or long and velvety?"

"I'm still confused over this situation. Tell me again why your mailman gave you an invitation to a vampire party." Alena was always suspicious of anything that nice people did for me. You give one Nigerian prince a few hundred dollars and suddenly your friends have to monitor your every move-ment. I could just picture Alena sitting in her kitchen, her concerned face surrounded by a cloud of shiny dark hair. Alena was one of those tall, naturally thin and effortlessly beautiful women that I normally resented at first sight. But because I'd known her since we were gawky teens, I'd gotten a gradual introduction to her brand of perfect beauty that was less jarring and easier to come to terms with.

"He has to work, Alena. Plus, Craig was rich once. He's already been to all these luxurious vampire soirees. He does-n't need to go to another one." Craig had been a rich vam-pire until the stock market tanked in 2008. At the time, Craig had everything in stocks and, just like that, he was left with nothing. Most vampires take an extremely long-term view when investing and leave all their assets in fixed-rate prod-ucts. After all, a three percent interest rate may not amount to much after ten or twenty years, but after one hundred to two hundred it looks pretty attractive. But Craig was a gam-bler and left everything in high-risk, speculative stocks that went south for the winter in 2008.

"He has to work-delivering the mail-at eight PM. I will never understand why the Americans with Disabilities Act pushed for these evening work laws," Alena snorted, then quoted the law with a tone of resentment. "'All employers must offer substantial shifts for evening workers.' Who needs their mail delivered at eight PM?" Alena was very resistant to change. Also, she sometimes had to work the midnight to 6 AM shift at the mortgage financing company she ran and she resented it. Actually, most humans resented the ADA's interference because most vampires didn't work so it was us who ended up working all of these crazy shifts.

Personally, I thought the new law was great. You could go to any store or restaurant at any time of night. Chinese food was delivered in the wee hours and banks had to be open 24/5. Have you ever gone through the bank drive-through at 2:31 AM? It's a rush.

"Alena, can we please get on track here? I've got to finish getting ready. Now I'll ask again, short and sparkly, or long and velvety?"

"How much cleavage on each of these dresses, Josie?"

Now, that wasn't really a fair question. When I was in grade school all the boys called me flatty because I was the last girl to develop a chest, but what they didn't know was that there was a rack with proportions bordering on obscene hiding under my flat-chested exterior, just biding its time before erupting from my chest. Combine them with my small waist and I was like a shorter, longer-haired, fouler-mouthed Mae West.

"Not a lot of cleavage, Alena. I don't want to be vulgar-just totally rip-my-dress-off-and-have-your-way-with-me hot."

"Okay, go for short and sparkly but wear your hair down. If you wear the long and velvety number you might be over-dressed, which would suck. Short and sparkly with long groomed hair can work for formal or casual."

"Right on-see, I knew you were the right person to call.

Fuck me, I'm so excited!"

"Josie, I have you on speakerphone."

Shit. Alena had been asking me for years, ever since she had her first baby, to stop swearing so her kids wouldn't pick it up. Shit.

"Alena, you have to tell Auntie Josie when you have her on speakerphone. Hi, Mason! Hi, Anthony!" The boys chorused back hellos, then I heard the older one, Mason, chanting something suspiciously similar to, "Fuck me, fuck me, fuck me."

"Great, I've got to go get some i-c-e-c-r-e-a-m to help the boys forget about Auntie Josie's dirty mouth. Have fun tonight and for my sake, please be careful."

"I will, mom. Talk to you tomorrow."

"You'd better."

When I hung up the phone I ran to the bed and held up short and sparkly. The dress was magnificent. I'd never had an occasion to wear it, but it was one of those dresses that you see and you simply have to buy, even if it does nothing but sit in your closet unworn for years.

It had spaghetti straps and was made out of some sort of stretchy material. It fit like a glove, but didn't look obscene because it was covered in these large silver sequins that softened my figure and helped avoid…well…looking slutty. The dress was short but then so am I. At five feet four inches even the shortest dresses end up a moderate length on me. Short and sparkly came down to rest about two inches above my knees, just short enough to show off some nice leg action.

Although I live in Florida and I absolutely adore lying out in the sun, I'm actually totally pale. The silver sequins on the dress had an undertone of blue that looked lovely with my pale skin and blue eyes. I was showing just enough cleavage but I did take a moment to be concerned about how very blue the veins in my breasts were with this dress on. All the better to attract vampires with, my pretty.

I slipped on a pair of Promiscuous pump sandals to complete the look. They were navy blue with the sweetest ruffles over the top of the foot and they complemented the dress perfectly. The three-inch heel didn't hurt the look of my leg either.

As Alena advised I left my curly blonde hair down. It reached the middle of my back so it covered a lot of skin and helped me look…well…you know-less slutty. I'm not an unattractive woman, but I'm not a movie star goddess either. If there is one thing truly remarkable about me (other than my rack) it is my hair. The soft ringlets gave my hair volume but they were touchable and sexy-not tight and small.

I added a simple pair of diamond earrings and a small purse and I was out the door to meet fate. No, wait, to meet destiny. That sounds more romantic.

CHAPTER 3

I walked up the highly polished steps outside the fashionable Beach Drive condo building with my heart in my mouth and my fear on my sleeve. Since I didn't actually have sleeves I guess the fear was on my arm, and let me tell you-it looked just like goose bumps. And on a ninety-five degree Florida evening with high humidity, goose bumps are an oddity.

Once inside the door I showed my invitation to the guard at the security desk. He gave it intense scrutiny, and then indicated that I should go up the curved marble staircase to my left and told me what condo number to look for. As I climbed the stairs the muffled noise of classy music became louder and clearer. I say classy music because it was just instruments and no vocals. You know, classy.

Eventually I reached the door of condo #J12. I lifted my hand to knock when the door suddenly opened and a woman about my age with short black hair wearing a basic black sheath stepped out. Her head was turned away from me as she talked to the guy following her. I stepped to the side and out of her way but not before she stumbled into me. Twisting her head around to discern what inferior being had the gall to block her passage, she quickly scanned me and gave me the evil eye.

If you speak Stink Eye as fluently as I do then you know that her evil eye meant I looked good. Real good. I straightened my back, pushed my tits forward, tilted my chin down, and pushed through the door that she had left slightly ajar.

Whatever I was expecting to see at a vampire party was forced out of my head as I walked in to the attractive loft. I was dressed perfectly, even a little better than some of the other women there. The men were dressed nicely but not too nicely. Many wore jeans with button-down shirts and sports coats and a few wore suits, sans ties. The music playing was some kind of jazz, and the lighting was amazing. It was warm, inviting, and just sort of glowed.

I walked into the living room, which was right off the tiny little foyer. The furniture was what you'd expect in any living room but it was brightly colored and minimalist style. The art on the wall looked like real art with the peaks and valleys that can only be created by oils.

Waiters, dressed in black pants with white shirts, circled with plates of tapas. Since I'd never been to a party with circulating waiters I got a little thrill in my tummy when one approached me. But then I realized that I didn't want to have stinky breath or food in my teeth before I got a chance to make a first impression on cute-single-vampire-McGee, so I just shook my head at the advancing waiter.

I didn't know anyone at the party, which made it really difficult to socialize. I don't know why I hadn't considered that before I actually got there, but there you have it. I just walked in, fell in love with the lighting, and then freaked out internally as I realized I didn't know how to start a conversation with a stranger.

I could easily pick out the vampires in the crowd because they were noticeably paler than the tanned humans and freakishly attractive. Here in the Sunshine State you can be pretty safe in your assumption that the pale people you meet are vampires, unless it's tourist season. I'm a pale human Floridian so I guess you can't be totally sure, but since tan is as "in" as thin, humans like me are a rarity.

I didn't want to start a conversation with a vampire yet; I wanted to practice on a human first. I decided to fall back on my retail roots and start a conversation about clothes or accessories with the first person I found standing alone.

"Nice cufflinks," I said to the tall, dark, and handsome loner leaning his elbows on the bar. Wait, did I say tall? Hah, that's an understatement. I mean looming-no, that sounds ominous. He was, well, he was impressive. He had to be six-foot-four or more. He was all muscle-but not too muscley. You knew just by looking at him that he was solidly built but it wasn't distracting.

He had dark hair cut in a messy, contemporary style. Not a stupid faux hawk but messy, thick, gorgeous clumps of dark man-hair. He was dressed in dark jeans, a white button down shirt unbuttoned at the neck, and a black sports coat. He also had on the cutest little ruby red teardrop-shaped cufflinks.

He moved his wrists to look at his cufflinks, almost like he wasn't sure which set he was wearing, then flashed me a gorgeous white smile. The teeth against his deep tan were startlingly bright, but not abnormally so. His eyes were dark, so dark they almost looked black, and they shined with interest, intelligence, and wit. My, my, he was yummy. Just as I was sort of mentally drifting off and considering how yummy other parts of him might be, he spoke.

"Thank you. They're a family heirloom. I'm Gregory Bullster and I don't think I've had the pleasure."

Shit. Of course the first person I decide to lose my party conversation cherry to and it has to be single, datable, male, attractive vampire Gregory. He grabbed my hand the wrong way for shaking and the right way for kissing and pulled it up to his lips, never once breaking eye contact with me.

"Josie," I sort of half sighed, half breathed. "My-my name is Josie."

He finished his too-hot-to-be-really-chaste kiss on my hand and said, "Josie, it's wonderful to meet you. How do I know you?" He didn't let go of my hand. His voice was so unique; it was like whiskey slipping over ice cubes.

"Oh, um, you don't-but your old friend Craig does. He told me to tell you hello. He couldn't make it-he has to work."

Gregory laughed a deep laugh. "Oh, Craig had to work. Let me guess, money problems forcing him to work an eight to five?"

"Something like that. Eight PM to five AM is more like it."

He looked at me with a still slightly bemused expression. "It's not surprising. Craig and I were once in business together and when we sold our company he put all of his proceeds into tech stocks which subsequently tanked. So what did he do now? Invest all of his money in more speculative stocks?"

"Well...pretty much."

Gregory laughed deeply and fully. A few people at the party turned to look at us. When he laughed, the corners of his eyes wrinkled in that sexy I'm-just-old-enough-to-know-more-than-you-in-the-bedroom way. Of course, Gregory was old enough to know about the original bird who'd had sex with a bee-or however that story went.

"Wait a minute," I realized, "you're tan. How are you tan?" I took in his flawless tan and wondered at how human and alive he looked thanks to the color.

"Airbrushed tanning is a wondrous thing. I keep encouraging other vampires to indulge but as yet, none have bothered. Do you like it?"

Did I like it. Plahahaha, mmmph. I'd have thought he was fishing for compliments if he didn't have a decidedly mischievous sparkle in his eyes. I think he was enjoying my discomfort as I sort of shifted my weight from foot to foot. "I guess you could say that I like it. It looks very natural. You don't look orange at all. Most people look like an Oompa-Loompa after an airbrush tan."

Again he laughed one of those full-throated laughs that made me seem much funnier than I actually was, and I got a little nervous. "I'm really not that funny, am I? I would blame your laughter on the alcohol being served tonight, but I'm not sure what kind of effect it has on you."

"No, you really are that funny. By now most women would be on a potential sex-and-sugar-daddy mission trying to find out what kind of car I drive, what my disposable income is, what kind of woman I'm interested in, and what my bedroom set's thread count is. You aren't doing any of those things and it's refreshing."

This time I laughed along with him. "Well, don't get the idea that I'm not a superficial, opportunistic vampire-humper simply from this conversation. This was all an attempt to lure you into complacency."

"Thank goodness, because I'm only interested in superficial, opportunistic vampire-humping women. Obviously, since this party is full of them." As he said this, he turned toward the room and snorted in disgust.

"Look at them," he continued. "All desperate to latch on to a vampire lover as if it's a status symbol. Vampires are people, not accessories."

I stood there, shocked at his raging humanity. Oh, that humanity. That sexy, luscious, heart-stopping humanity. I had no idea vampires felt that way and honestly, I felt a little guilty about objectifying them myself.

"You know, Gregory, I know exactly what you mean about women using vampire lovers as status symbols because that's what men usually do to chicks. Do you know how many men I talk to in a day who can actually tell you my eye color? Pah, you'd have a better shot asking them to estimate my cup size."

He stared intensely into my eyes and I couldn't tell if he was angry or...well, I guess angry. His gaze was heated and a little frightening. "Josie, any man who doesn't look you in the eye is not worth your time. You are a beautiful, funny, intelligent woman and you deserve to be treated that way. Men who are interested only in your physical allure are missing out on a truly remarkable person."

I was wary, but I gave in to the possible sincerity of the compliment. Sure, he'd only met me about five minutes ago but hell, he'd been alive hundreds of years. I'm sure character judgment was a finely honed skill by now. "Thank you, Gregory, that really means a lot." I paused, thinking I should probably end this conversation on a high note before I said something to make him think that I wasn't funny and intelligent after all. "I feel like I'm taking up too much of your time though. I should leave you so you can circulate."

"Do you have to? I despise these parties and I loathe circulating." He glanced around the room with a look of annoyance.

"If you hate these parties then why have them?"

"Do you know much about the Vampire Handbook?" His voice lowered slightly and his head bent closer to mine.

"A handbook? You need a handbook? No, what is up with the handbook?"

"It's more of a code of conduct. Because vampires live for so long there are certain rules that we've developed for ourselves."

"Dude, if your rules involve required party throwing then I'd have to say that's the coolest rule book ever."

"Ah, Josie, if only it were so simple. The Handbook dictates our hierarchical structure. It's treated by your government as the guide of a fraternal group, but in reality it's a vampire government. "

"Wait," I interrupted him. "You have your own mini-government? And the federal, human one doesn't mind?"

"That is correct. Vampires are magical creatures and cannot be entirely controlled within the constraints of human law. Our government acts as a supporting government to your own but with special rules that allow us to enforce laws and punish vampires on a level they will better respect."

"I still don't understand. I mean, why can't our government and legal system punish vampires enough to make them behave?"

"Between our strength, which is greater than a human's

but greatly exaggerated by modern literature, and our blood-sucking capabilities, it's very difficult for human law enforcement officers and courts to contain and enforce our kind. Instead, we have a system of vampire governors and law enforcers who keep the vampire population under control."

"Okay, so I get your spooky hierarchy and ominous punishment deal, but what does that have to do with throwing parties against your will?" And then it dawned on me. Gregory was obviously some sort of criminal. "Oh, wait, is being forced to throw a party against your will a punishment for something? Is it like in *1984* when they put rats in Winston's face? The vampire law enforcers just take your worst fear and make you live it as punishment?"

Gregory looked at me for a moment and then burst into one of his deep laughing fits again. "Oh, Josie, you are too much. You are an interesting mix of sophisticated wit and innocent naïveté. No, I'm not being punished. Law enforcers are chosen by vampire vote. I am a law enforcer and my position is up for re-election in a few weeks. If there's one thing vampire society has in common with human society, it is that parties sway voters."

I would have felt worse if he hadn't made my naïveté sound almost endearing. "So this is the part of your campaign where you hold babies, shake hands, and take pictures with the adoring crowd, eh?"

"Exactly. I can never wait until it's over, though." He was taking a sip of the pink wine he'd been drinking when we were interrupted by a short human with a buzz cut. He was in his mid-fifties and his stomach was so large that it was hiking his pants up, offering everyone a glimpse of his argyle socks.

"Say, Gregory, you got a minute? I've been having some trouble down at the shop, you know? I was wondering if we could discuss the whole VC issue for a minute," said the short, argyle sock-wearing man with no apology for interrupting my amazing conversation.

"Lewis, of course. Excuse me, Josie-duty calls. It's been a pleasure." He gazed at me intensely and grabbed my hand. He brought it once again to his lips and I shivered.

As my hand dropped back to my side and I turned away from Gregory, I couldn't help feeling saddened that I hadn't gotten his phone number or given him mine. But then, there were plenty of other hot vampires at the party.

Strangely, none of them seemed quite as hot anymore.

CHAPTER 4

As I moved along into the throng of partygoers, a woman grabbed my elbow and turned me slightly to face her. She was about my height, human, and her face was covered in so much makeup it looked like she might have carved her features out after applying it. She squinted her eyes and gave me a quick appraisal and then asked, "Are you trying to get in his pants?"

"To whom's pants do you think I am trying to get in?" I've never been certain when I should or shouldn't use whom or who, and since I wanted to seem powerful and important I thought I should throw it in there just in case.

"Don't bullshit me, girlie. Are you trying to get into Gregory's pants? Because if you are, you will regret it. You're not his type and he's a notorious playboy. He uses women and then throws them away. He tells them what they want to hear, plays with their hearts, then moves on to the next one in line."

Outraged, I asked the question that was begging to be asked, "What do you mean I'm not his type?"

"Oh, you silly, immature girl. Fine, do as you wish. But don't say I didn't warn you."

"When you say that, do you mean that I should someday say that you did, actually, warn me or that I should make sure to never say that you avoided warning me? Because saying that you never warned me would be ridiculous since you obviously have and I'm not sure why you think you need to give me instructions not to do that." I smiled inside at my never-ending ability to confound people with my seeming stupidity.

She dropped my arm and looked at me like I'd grown four new heads. Then, as if waking herself out of her own daydream, she shook her head and walked away. Since my party experience definitely seemed to be headed downhill I decided to check out.

I made my way to the door when someone tapped me on the shoulder. I turned to see a waiter with a tray of tapas. "Dude, I'm leaving and I don't think I need any tapas to go."

He looked confused and hesitated. "Josie?"

"Yuppers."

"Ah, Mr. Bullster asked me to give this to you." He took a business card out of his pocket and handed it to me. I took it and he remained standing there, so I pulled the card up to my face and read it. The front of the card had Gregory's business telephone and email and on the back was a hand-written cell phone number along with a request for me to give the waiter my number.

I glanced away from the waiter and saw Gregory facing my direction. He was nodding his head at the vampire standing in front of him but his eyes were reaching out to me from across the room. That was the only encouragement I needed. I pulled my eyeliner pencil out of my purse and grabbed the waiter's hand. I wrote my number on his palm and then realized that the waiter could get sweaty and my number would be reduced to black smudge.

I looked up at him and said in my most entitled and menacing voice, "Now you see that you transfer this number to paper post-haste or Mr. Bullster over there is going to get all fangy over you."

The waiter looked frightened and pulled back, then ran toward the kitchen holding his empty hand high above his head.

CHAPTER 5

I left the party feeling mighty fine and a whistle was on my lips to illustrate my fineness. My mother hates it when I whistle. She says it's not ladylike, though why she'd waste her breath on trying to make me a lady was anyone's guess. I walked outside and was greeted by the smell of salt water and the wet, oppressive blanket known as high humidity. Since we were downtown, the buzz of cars dueled with the click of the cicadas. Above all that I could hear the warm Florida breeze rustling through the tall palm trees. I headed to my car, the heels of my shoes making a hollow clicking noise as they beat the pavement into submission.

When I reached my car I noticed a tall vampire standing near Gregory's building, lighting a cigarette. I glanced over at him, trying to get a peek at his face. He was a little skinnier than I usually like my men, but he had an oddly graceful sexiness about him. He had shoulder length, dark blond hair that was layered and brushed his cheekbones in the front. He was wearing all black-black boots, black pants, black shirt, black trench coat. The outfit would have been out of place on a human but since vamps ran cold I completely understood.

I must've stared at him a little too long because he looked at me and made that half scrunchy face that smokers make where one eye squints and their mouth puckers up and moves over to settle on that side of the face. He put his thumb and his forefinger to his lips and pulled out the cigarette.

"What are you looking at?" he asked as he blew nasty cigarette smoke in my direction. His voice was sexy raspy like you'd expect from a Marlboro-smoking dude ranch worker and it sent shivers up my spine. He wasn't really rude when he said it, but there was a confrontational feeling about him.

"Oh, uh, sorry. I...I've just never seen a vampire smoke. You guys don't even breathe, do you?"

He made a sound that was like a laugh but not like a ha-ha-let's-share-a-joke kind of laugh. "You just came from a party with vampires in it and you don't even know if we breathe? Do you pay attention to anything that happens *around* you, or only what happens *to* you?"

I was pretty offended by this asshole vampire, but I couldn't really argue his point. After all, I did just come from a party full of vampires but wasn't actually sure whether or not they breathed. Then I remembered Gregory's sigh. "Oh yeah, I guess you guys do breathe."

"Oh yeah," he mocked my feminine lilt. "And we have hearts and *everything*."

I looked at him for a minute, trying to come up with an impressive and damaging insult, but all I could make my mouth say was, "Screw you, asshole."

I reached into my purse to get my keys out and was so flustered that the little mirror I keep in my purse to check my lipstick fell out and shattered. "Damn it, look what you made me do! I've had that mirror for years and within five minutes of meeting you it's shattered."

"Wow, guess you just bought yourself seven years of bad luck there, diva."

I gave him one last glare, got in my car, and left, realizing that my party experience had finally crashed to the bottom of that downward slope.

CHAPTER 6

I woke up the next morning to the obnoxiousness that is "Flight of the Bumblebee" because I had forgotten to turn my cell phone off when I got in the night before. I picked up the phone with a grumbled, "What?"

"Josie, this is Megan. Can you come in today? Sadie called in sick." It was my boss. Shit.

"Uh, sure, Megan, what time?" I didn't want to go in, no, I sure didn't. Especially on a Saturday, which, in a bridal shop, is like but with brides coming at you from every direction instead of zombies.

Like zombies, brides have one thing on their mind. "Perfect dress," they drone with the same mesmerized but insistent tone favored by the living dead in a George Romero film. And make no mistake, those brides will eat your brain if you don't make them look thirty pounds thinner and at least five years younger in a one-of-a-kind but completely affordable miracle dress that doesn't exist. But I could use the money and it would be real hard for my brain to come up with a believable excuse for avoiding work when I'd just come directly out of a dream about a giant taco wearing ballet shoes.

"Great. Be there at eight to open the store." And then she hung up. Naturally. No thank-yous or anything.

I pulled my hair back into a low-maintenance ponytail, put on one of my many iron-free skirt suits and a pair of sensible heels, and drove in to work. Once I got to the shop I fished my keys out of my purse and opened up the employee entrance. I put my purse away in my locker and headed out to the floor to start greeting the brides.

The day progressed pretty normally. Before I knew it, I was up to my elbows in tulle, lace, garters, and crinoline. By six o'clock, as the sun was starting its descent, I was eagerly awaiting the time that I'd be able to rip off my shoes and settle in to a Chevy Chase movie rerun.

Just as dark had overtaken the parking lot I noticed that Pink Tulle Nightmare Bride was back and she was pulling the same pink tulle dress off the rack. When brides come by the first time, it's like window shopping. They're just looking, trying stuff on, getting the feel of your stock. When they come in the second time you can be pretty certain that they've made their final decision on a dress.

Normally, it doesn't matter to me whether or not the dress the bride picks looks stunning to me while she's wearing it because, hey-it's her wedding. But in this case, the Pink Tulle Nightmare looked ridiculous on the lady and I felt like I really needed to be a good person and talk her out of it.

"Oh, Ms. Simpson, how wonderful to see you again! I was thinking of calling you because we got a new dress in since the last time you were here. It's an ivory A-line that would look amazing on you."

"Why would I want to look at another dress? You can see that I'm reaching for this B. Mack Original again. Obviously this is the one that I want."

Now this was tricky business. I certainly couldn't tell her that she looked like a tulle-covered hemorrhoid when wearing that dress, but I still felt I owed her the truth-even if only by way of misdirection. "Oh, I see that, and it is a gorgeous dress, but this ivory dress would really complement your complexion. Don't you want to at least try it on?"

"If I didn't know better," she looked at me with squinted eyes and twisted her body into a defensive posture over the dress, "I'd think you were trying to talk me out of this dress."

It was at this moment that my boss, Megan, decided to interject. "Josie, Ms. Simpson, is there a problem here?"

"I'll say there's a problem." Ms. Simpson turned to Megan. "This one," she said, pointing at me, "is trying to stop me from buying this dress." She accentuated every word with a little tug on the dress of her dreams.

Megan turned to me and said, "Josie, maybe you should go to the back and take a break."

Christ, now I was in trouble just for trying to do something nice. I turned around and started to huff back to the employee area when I noticed a tall column of black to my left. What do you know, it was cigarette squinty from outside Gregory's party last night.

He grabbed my arm gently as I walked by and whispered, "I need to apologize to you. Is there somewhere we could talk?"

"Sure, but if you're going to apologize I'll need you to do it with a regular voice so I can really hear the words," I stage whispered back to him. "Follow me."

He laughed and let go of my arm as I led him outside.

Once we were outside the shop I turned around, crossed

my arms, and started tapping my foot. For the first time, I noticed that he had green eyes. Not emerald green, but more like an absorbent olive green.

He looked me up and down, slowly, eyes lingering over all the areas that a gentleman doesn't linger over. I let that go on for, oh, about three seconds before I decided to redirect. "Um, hi, yeah, sorry to interrupt your retinal foreplay but are you going to apologize or what?"

His eyes stopped moving but they stayed on my breasts as he delivered his speech, his gruff, grumbly voice sending shivers up and down my spine. "Josie, I am utterly regretful that I was so rude to you outside the magnificent gala we both attended last night." Then he moved his eyes to meet mine. "I do hope you can forgive my nicotine withdrawal-induced rudeness."

"That has got to be the worst apology I've ever heard. Seriously, worst ever, and a lot of people have apologized to me over the course of my life, Nicotine-o, a lot."

"Apologized to you because you are a self-indulgent little pouter or because they actually wronged you?"

"Okay, you know what? Fuck off. Thanks for stopping by my work to waste the oxygen that hovers around me with your non-apology, dickweed." I threw my hands up and started to walk off, then I turned. "How the fuck did you find out where I work? And how do you know my name?"

"Oh, please, don't look at me that way. I'm not a stalker and if I were, it wouldn't be you I'd stalk, Señorita Ego. I talked to Gregory when I went back to the party and your name was mentioned, so it wasn't exactly rocket science to find you."

"Well, maybe it won't be rocket science to un-find me

then, asswipe. Apology not accepted." Then I turned on him and as I walked back in, I thought I heard the distinct sound of soft laughter.

PART 2 – SCORING A DATE WITH A VAMPIRE

*D*ear Editor,

The article by Remis Strogan about letting the vampires make the first move was dead-on. After all, vampires are very traditional and they hate the modern woman's aggressive dating tactics. Thank you for printing such an informative article.

—Letter to the Editor printed in *V Magazine*

CHAPTER 7

Four days later I was sitting on the porch of my cottage. When I say cottage, I make it sound way more romantic than it actually is. I live in a small rental cottage that would once have been called a mother-in-law's suite. It's like a tiny little shed with windows behind my landlord's house. The cottage itself is about 450 square feet with a small kitchen, a dining area, sleeping nook, and bathroom. It's perfect for me because I really don't want that much space to clean.

So there I was on the porch in an Adirondack chair looking at my landlord's night-blooming jasmine and thinking about my vampire flirtation experiment and how much my flirtation skills must have sucked because while the one vampire I was rude to made it a point to come all the way to my workplace to bother me, the vampire I had actually tried to flirt with hadn't even called. Since I had my cordless phone outside with me and enough liquid courage in the form of hard lemonade, I decided to call Gregory and remind him of the fun we'd had talking at his party. I fished his number out of my purse and let my finger do the walking.

I'd be lying by omission if I didn't admit that I really just wanted to reach his answering machine.

"Hullo?" His deep voice slipped over my body like hot chocolate on cold ice cream.

"Hi, Gregory, this is Josie. We met at your party the other night?"

He sounded surprised to hear from me but not unhappy-a good sign...I think... "Oh, Josie-I was going to call you when I got back."

"Back?"

"Yes. I'm out of the country on business. I was going to call you tomorrow when I got back in and ask you on a date. Oh, but maybe you've beaten me to the punch?" He had a sort of teasing tone, as if he didn't think I'd actually ask him on a date. Thirty years' worth of lectures about feminism reared its ugly head and I decided that I'd surprise the sexy bastard and throw him off his game.

"As a matter of fact, I was calling to ask you to go on a date with me Saturday."

"My, my. In about eight hundred years you are the first woman to ever ask me out on a date. So, where will you be taking me on this illustrious occasion?"

I was a little miffed at the humor in his tone, but it was my own impatience that got me into this feminist nightmare, so I'd have to deal with the consequences. But maybe there was still a way that I could keep the upper hand. "Oh, just the usual. Bowling followed by dinner at a quaint Italian restaurant."

"Bowling?" He said it slowly, as if trying to decide whether or not he liked the taste of it in his mouth.

"Yuppers, bowling. Make sure you wear socks-those rental shoes can get nasty. Not that you can get an infection or anything, since you're a vampire, but...they're still nasty.

What time should I pick you up?" I hated bowling, but it would be worth it, rented shoes and all, just to see Gregory's rich, hot, 800-year-old vampire ass at a bowling alley.

Gregory laughed his deep, velvety laugh and sounded like he was genuinely interested in the date. "I can't wait, this sounds like quite the treat. I'll be ready at eight."

"I'm looking forward to it. See you then." We each hung up.

CHAPTER 8

"You asked him out?" I was at work the following evening telling my co-worker Sadie the story of my phone call to Gregory while she was wrestling with the steam iron. I shouldn't have distracted her but it was funny watching her try to de-wrinkle a devastatingly expensive wedding gown, avoid singeing the silk shantung, and call me out on vampire dating hubris.

"Yes, yes, I did. After all, why should I have to sit on my hands for weeks until he decides to call?"

"But Josie, didn't it make you feel like he wasn't really interested? It seems to me that if he was interested in getting to know you, he would have called. Maybe now he's just going out with you because he feels bad?"

"No, he was out of town. He…he would have called, I know he would have."

Sadie opened her mouth to argue more when the bell above the shop's front door jangled and indicated that a customer had walked in. It was Thursday night, not a big wedding gown shopping night, but I hustled out there anyway, glad to have been spared more of Sadie's self-esteem shattering observations.

As I walked out from the back room I quickly scanned the shop to see where the customer went when, for the second time in five days, a column of black caught my eye. In a bridal shop filled with white gowns, someone wearing all black stands out. I also caught the faint smell of stale cigarettes.

"You."

"Why, hello, Señorita Ego! How I've missed your engaging repartee." He was standing by the dressing rooms with his hands held behind his back and he started walking toward me, his dark blond hair still in that long, sexy style.

"This is twice in one week you've been to my work, weirdo stalker, and I don't even know your name."

He reached me and was close enough to touch but kept his hands behind his back. "Hmmm, that's interesting. Do you want to know my name?"

For the first time, I looked at Nicotine-o. I mean, I really looked at him. He was definitely a vampire, just as perfect as they always are, but there was something different about his eyes. They were somehow more soulful. They were amused on the surface but when I looked deeper I could see anger, sadness, pain, an entire lifetime of rich experience. It made him seem more three-dimensional than Gregory and I softened to him.

"Yes."

"Well, I don't know you well enough yet to give you my real name, but you can call me Walker."

"Do other people call you Walker, or is this just what I get to call you?"

"Other people sometimes call me Walker."

"Why are you so vague and shady, oh vampire that sometimes, some people, occasionally call Walker?"

He laughed. "There, now that's the Josie I'm comfortable with. The Josie that's immediately defensive, extremely impolite, and has to make a big deal out of everything. Oh, how I've missed you these past few minutes."

Now he had me chuckling-after all, he was sort of right. "What do you want, Smokey? Either make me a commission or scoot on back to the bat cave you call home."

His arms came from around his back to show me a single tulip. He handed it to me. "I'd like to ask you out to dinner Sunday."

I was flabbergasted, which might explain the answer I gave him. "Uh…okay."

He looked at me oddly. "I thought surely it would be harder than this. Josie, are you feeling all right?" Just then he put his hand on my forehead as if to check for a fever. The moment that his cool, smooth but firm hand touched my forehead I felt a jolt of electricity that reached right down into my libido, tugged at the beast, woke him, and then ran away. Judging by the way his eyes widened slightly, I think Nicotine-o felt it too.

I backed away out of the potentially dangerous touch-zone. "I feel fine, Nicotine-o. Where are you taking me Sunday? What fast food joint should I ready my digestive system for?"

He laughed. "Well, Josie, as you can imagine, with me it's all about style. We'll be going to Rocket Burger for bike night."

"You're kidding, right? Rocket Burger, on bike night, for a first date?" Rocket Burger was a fifty-year-old burger joint and bar that hosted classic auto and motorcycle nights. It was loud, not terribly clean, and not the best place to bring a first date.

"Nope. Not kidding. I'll pick you up at eight." At that, he started toward the door.

"Wait, how do you know where I live?"

He turned around and looked at me for a moment, then said, "There's a lot that I know about you, Josie." Then he left.

PART 3 – GOING ON A DATE WITH A VAMPIRE

Dear Vampy,

I'm going out on my first date with a vampire next week and I'm not sure what dating "rules" might be different for vampires than for humans. Can you help?

—Susan R. in Minnesota

Dear Susan,

Girl, please. Vampire dating rules are not to be compared with the rules of paltry humans. We live for thousands of years. A date to us is like the blink of an eye to you. Do you have rules for the time you spend blinking? Of course not. Throw all your usual rules out the window for your date and just hang on for the ride.

—Excerpt from the syndicated *Dear Vampy* column

CHAPTER 9

First date Saturday (as I had taken to calling it) came around much more quickly than I felt ready for but I was totally excited to see Gregory again. Since we were going bowling I decided to wear jeans. I would have worn capris but if I did and then had to don socks and bowling shoes with them I would look like Sarah Jessica Parker from her *Square Pegs* days, and that was not exactly the look I was going for. Since Florida is hot about ninety percent of the time, I paired the jeans with a lacey camisole and strappy sandals. I left my hair down and added a pendant that nestled between my breasts. I looked totally doable.

I bought some flowers at a crappy gas station on my way to pick up Gregory. They were supposed to be fresh carnations, but they looked like the day-old special to me. But because I had waited until the last moment for this detail, I had no choice but to take the stale, wilty bouquet.

When I got to his condo building I was a nervous wreck. At the party we had been surrounded by people and distractions. There was no pressure and there were certainly no expectations. Now, it would just be Gregory and me and all of my pressures and expectations-and any he might have too.

Once I passed the scrutiny of the security guard I mounted the stairs slowly, wiping my sweaty hands off on my jeans. I'd never been on this end of the date before, and it wasn't pretty. I had a newfound respect for the entire male species. I reached Gregory's door and lifted my hand to knock but before I got the chance the door sprung open.

I pushed the flowers in front of me and toward Gregory almost like they were the perfect physical barrier to prevent an unexpected hug. For someone who desperately wanted to try sex with a vampire I was acting awfully wimpy. Gregory looked shocked and more than a little bit amused to be receiving flowers, and when he took them from me I realized he was pushing a bouquet of long-stemmed pink roses back in my direction.

"What? You got me flowers? But Gregory, I'm the dater and you're the datee-you are the only one who should be getting flowers!" His bouquet was much more beautiful than mine, and probably much more expensive. But then, he'd probably never received flowers from a girl before so he had nothing to really compare it too.

"A beautiful woman should always be in receipt of flowers. But, this is a night of surprises. I've never received flowers from a woman before." See, told you. "These are lovely, Josie, let me put them in some water." He winked at me deliciously as though he knew how ironic he was being.

He walked into the kitchen and brought out two vases, filled them with water, unwrapped the bouquets, cut all the stems at an angle, and placed them both in the vases. I took this time to survey the vampire goods. Gregory looked unbelievably hot. His short, thick, dark hair was carefully mussed as it had been the night I met him. He had on a pair of dark-washed jeans that were distressed in all the right places along with a white button-down shirt that made his tan look even more dark and sexy. I was about to play *Guess What Underwear Your Date is Wearing* when his voice brought me back to reality. "When you come up for your nightcap you can retrieve your flowers." He gave me another delicious wink.

"Holding little floral hostages so that you can get a good-night kiss?" I might have been doing a happy dance on the inside, but I decided that I shouldn't seem too eager on the outside.

He laughed. "Whatever it takes, my lovely, whatever it takes." He finished with the flowers and took my hand. It was a casual handhold, like two people who had been dating for months, and he led me out the door.

When we got to the car I opened the door for him. I was a little worried that he might see this as emasculating rather than playful, but he seemed to really be enjoying this role reversal.

I walked around to the driver's side of my white Eclipse and as I got in I noticed Gregory was looking through my glove compartment. "Wow, a little nosy, aren't we?"

"Well, I don't think I am. I was just looking for a tissue…and a stake."

"Huh? Why are you looking in my glove compartment for a steak? I'm taking you out to dinner-but wait, you don't eat steak anyway. Or wait-I have seen vampires eat normal food, so maybe you will eat a steak." Secretly, I really hoped he wouldn't because I didn't exactly have a restaurant-steak kind of budget.

He laughed and closed my glove compartment. "No, no, a wooden stake. It's a safety precaution in case you are an anti-vampire zealot."

Wow. He really thinks I have, like, thoughts and stuff. "Um, no. I'm a fan, I swear. So it's true then that a wooden stake is the way to kill a vampire?"

He looked at me strangely, which I guess is how I'd look at someone I was dating who asked, on said date, if a certain weapon would kill me. "Well, used the right way it certainly could. Generally, vampires can be killed in much the same way that any person can be killed. We do tend to heal better than humans, but we can still be killed if an injury is bad enough."

After an uncomfortable silence, we made small talk as I drove. Finally, we reached our sexy date locale, the Sunset Bowling Lanes. The neon sign atop the building was pink and blue and half of the neon letters and pictures were out so that only the ball and one pin were lit. I tried to rush out of my car to open his side for him but he didn't wait and opened his own door. Then we raced each other to the front of the bowling alley, each of us trying to gently elbow the other out of the way in order to get ahead and open the door for the other. It was like romance on the offensive. We laughed and I felt like we were connecting in a good way.

"You know, you really have a beautiful laugh." Gregory gazed at me and his face turned serious. He'd won the fight over the door and we were standing there, elbows out, with the door handle in his hands and my body twisted so that I was facing him with my left elbow in front of his stomach and my right arm closer to his back. He let go of the door to the bowling alley and put that arm around my waist along with his other arm and pulled me closer. His gaze flicked between my lips and my eyes as he moved his head down. He lightly pressed his lips against mine and gave me a sensuous, silky kiss. His lips were soft like velvet and not wet. He kept his tongue behind the barrier of his lips which I was sad about, but for a first kiss I guess it was appropriate. Also, it was super nice to get that over with so that we didn't have it hanging over our heads all night. It's a fact: ninety percent of first dates fail due to first kiss preoccupation (once again, I have anecdotal evidence to prove this).

The angry yelling of a pissed off bowler with a nicotine addiction took us out of the moment. The man was desperate to get out of the alley and light up but Gregory and I were blocking his passage to lung cancer. I blushed and moved away, making eye contact with the parking lot tar while Gregory pulled the door open for the man. The smoker bustled out, grumbling under his breath as he tried to light his cigarette. Gregory made a hand motion indicating that I should go inside and I slipped through the door he held open.

I wasn't sure if Gregory had ever been in a bowling alley before. He looked around with a mixture of awe, wonder, and disgust in his eyes. I tried to see the room as he might. While listening to the bang and pounding of bowling balls hitting the lanes and crashing into pins I saw overweight, drunk men licking grease and salt off their oil-stained fingers and guffawing over jokes that I couldn't hear. I saw the kids in the little arcade to the right of the lanes trying to beat the top score on some kind of shooter game. I noticed the teenagers making out sloppily in a darkened crevice by the shoe counter.

We walked up to the counter with all the dilapidated, pre-worn shoes lined up on the wall and bought ourselves a lane. We each rented a pair of shoes and then we went to sit in front of the "Lane of Possibilities," as I quickly named the area. When I got ready to put on my nasty rented shoes, Gregory decided to help me get my sandals off. I pulled my socks out of my purse as Gregory took my left foot in his hand and rested it on his thigh. His fingertips brushed my ankles delicately as he unclasped the small buckle on my sandal and chills of sexy anticipation flowed up my leg and into my breasts. No really, they frickin' did. He slowly pulled off my sandal once he had it unhitched and I took my foot back to put my sock on. Then he grabbed my other foot and repeated the action.

I wasn't sure if I was supposed to reciprocate and grab his shoes to remove them, but since I'm not a big fan of feet, I opted not to. I did want him to know that his attentions were appreciated so I stood up and put my hand on his shoulder and rubbed slowly and lightly, like a glimpse of the touching that was to come. He looked up at me, stopped fussing with his shoe, and put his hand around my waist to pull me closer to him. He was tall, even sitting, and his face was eye-level to my chest but he kept his eyes turned up to mine. I realized at that point that I could seriously be happy just spending all my days doing nothing but being touched by him.

"Do you want anything to drink?" I asked.

"Actually, I could use some blood. O negative if they have it."

I disengaged myself from his hands and walked toward the bar. Blood for vampires is served everywhere, but since

I didn't think vampires frequented bowling alleys, I wasn't sure what to expect. While I had seen blood on menus at all types of restaurants, I hadn't ever watched a vampire actually drink it. Vampires didn't seem to spend much time sitting at the Applebee's bar next to me.

The whole drinking blood thing is not as creepy as you might think. Blood is harvested from human donors, like those who donate to the Red Cross. Vampire blood collection buses go to office buildings, malls, and any other place frequented by crowds and collect blood from volunteers to package and resell to grocery stores, restaurants, and convenience stores. They pay the volunteers pretty well and have very strict regulations about how often you can give so that no one becomes too depleted.

I reached the bar and got the attention of the bartender. It wasn't a busy night but he was distracted by a small television behind the bar that was playing some sort of sport highlight thing. I don't know what sport; there were sticks and balls and men in tight clothing involved, though. I ordered a Mojito for myself and asked for Gregory's O negative. The bartender handed me the blue bag of blood and, since this was the first time I'd ever seen one, much less held one in my hand, I took a moment to look it over. It reminded me a bit of a Capri Sun, but it was long and thin, almost like an ear of corn. On the top, right in the middle, was a four-inch rectangle of foil.

"Do you have any straws or anything for this?" I asked the bartender, thinking this might be used like a juice box.

He raised an eyebrow and considered me for a moment. "That's how they come, right like that. No straws or nothin'."

"Well, can I have a glass?" Gregory didn't seem like the kind of vampire who'd want to drink out of the package.

"Listen, lady, I don't know how long you've been hanging out with the vampires but take it from me, they don't want no straws or no glasses." At that he turned back around to look at his television and started drying glasses. I left the money for the drinks on the counter (a ridiculous amount, I might add) and brought them back to our lane.

As I handed Gregory his drink and sat down at our little lane table, I thought about all the volunteers who had been paid to comprise his meal. I started to get icked out over the thought that the blood could be the mixed result of the pooling of several volunteers' donations but stopped myself as I realized that a hamburger could be the pooling of several abused, factory farm cows who had definitely not volunteered, but that sure didn't stop me from indulging in a bovine patty on occasion.

Then I watched as Gregory's fangs descended and he popped them through the foil while holding the sides of the blood bag. As I watched him I realized that there was no way he was actually drinking this blood. Only his teeth had gone through the foil.

I must have been staring too long because Gregory suddenly smirked. He stopped…uh…drinking and asked, "Are you curious about something, Josie?"

"Well, actually, yeah. It doesn't look like you're drinking the blood, although I can see the bag getting that sucked in look. But, how is the blood getting to your stomach?"

"While we all use the terms 'eat' and 'drink' to describe our taking of blood, we aren't actually drinking or eating it. A vampire's teeth have small canals, or tubes, in them much like a snake's. We simply take the blood up these canals and it enters our bloodstream."

I was starting to get squicked out again. Eager to change the subject, I looked down on the table in front of the "Lane of Possibilities" and searched for the score cards. "Are you keeping score? Because I hate doing that," I asked him.

He pointed toward a computer on the lane's table and said, "I think they take their own score, we just have to put our names in, which I will gladly take care of."

That settled, I walked-no, I sauntered. I definitely sauntered and tried like hell to make those nasty ass bowling shoes look hot. Ahem, I sauntered over to the wall of balls and picked out a small pink ball that wasn't too heavy. I walked back and positioned myself in front of the lane and then threw the ball down the waxy wooden course. It bounced. Twice. I got a few dirty looks, not the least of which was from the guy behind the shoe rental counter.

I heard Gregory softly laughing behind me. He had chosen his ball when I got the blood and Mojito. I took my next shot, this one gentler, and enjoyed the Zen-like sensation of watching a gutter ball make its way toward nowhere and nothing. It was like the sound of one hand trying to clap but not succeeding.

I skulked back to the table and gave the still laughing Gregory a dirty look as he passed me to take his turn. Since I assumed this 800-year-old vampire had never been bowling, I figured it'd be my turn to laugh shortly.

Gregory threw the ball down the aisle with perfect bowler's posture. His right leg swept, on point, behind his left. He made a strike. Son of a...

He turned to look at me, still with that sparkle in his eye, as I sat at the table with my arms crossed over my chest, and I gave him the nastiest look I could muster. The game didn't last very long. Gregory creamed my ass.

We returned our shoes and balls and walked out (hand in hand) to my car. On the way to the car, I noticed Gregory looking around the parking lot with a sort of hyperawareness.

"Is something wrong?" I thought about his searching my glove box for a stake and wondered if anti-vamp zealots were a common occurrence.

"No, no. I always like to familiarize myself with my surroundings." He patted our clasped hands with his other hand and then we separated as he walked around to his side of the car.

I drove Gregory to Sausalito's, an Italian restaurant that I love. Once there, we were seated in an intimate corner. It looked to me like Gregory had "greased the palm" of the maitre d', which was super cool and made me feel like I was in the movie *Goodfellas*. I ordered the baked ziti and Italian bread along with some red wine and Gregory ordered another liquid blood and…grrr, steak (rare), damn it. Guess I wasn't going to buy those new shoes I had my eyes on.

You might think that bringing a vampire to an Italian restaurant is a bad idea, what with all the garlic, but this restaurant, like many others, had a vampire friendly menu. Kind of like a kid's menu but with foods that humans could eat that would not offend or kill a vampire who tried for a goodnight kiss. That means that the food on the vampire friendly menu was Italian but had no garlic or onions.

I'd gotten used to seeing these menus over the years, but since Gregory had been nice enough to explain the inner workings of his vampire teeth to me, I wondered if he could answer some questions I had about their inability to eat onions and garlic. "Gregory, can I ask you a question?"

"Of course, Josie."

"Why can't vampires be around onions and garlic?"

"Well, much like cats, vampires can't *ingest* garlic or onions although we can smell them without harm. But if the juice of a garlic clove or onion is rubbed onto a person's skin and a vampire bites them, the vampire is in for a nasty and deadly surprise because in both cats and vampires a component of garlic and onions works to destroy red blood cells and causes a special kind of anemia."

"But people have anemia all the time and they just take iron pills for it. Why would that be deadly to vampires?"

"A vampire's blood is part blood and part magic. But something must be forsaken for the magic to come into the mix. Vampires, therefore, have forsaken the ability to create red blood cells. In a normal human, like you, red blood cells die every hundred twenty or so days, but your body retains the ability to create new ones. Since our bodies don't, we need the equivalent of a full person's blood every one hundred twenty days. Instead of draining an entire person every four months, we drink a little bit of blood each day. That gives us the equivalent of an entire person in a rotating one-twenty-day cycle."

"So, anemia adding further destruction of red blood cells would be really, really fucked up, right?"

Gregory chuckled. "Exactly. If a vampire were to ingest garlic or onions their death would not be immediate, but it would gradually occur as the anemia weakened their system irreparably."

The conversation and fun had been flowing pretty easily between us all night, but for some reason, when the waiter brought our food, I got a little nervous. Gregory reached across the table and slid his hand over mine. His hand was cool and smooth. Not ice cold because he did have some warmed blood flowing through his veins from the bowling alley, but it was definitely on the cool side. "I have had a wonderful time tonight," he said.

"Oh, you sound surprised."

He laughed. "Well, maybe I am. I didn't know what to expect giving up control of the first date."

"First date…hmmm…that seems to indicate there will be others."

He looked at me very seriously. The good-natured twinkle in his eye was still there but it had changed into something more serious. His hand squeezed mine slightly-not at all to hurt but to create a more intense form of contact. "If I have anything to say about it, it will be the first of many."

We were having a great date, no question about that, but I didn't understand why Gregory was so intense. It was like he was trying to turn the feelings that occur on a first date into those developed after months of dating. As a vampire who was, for all intents and purposes, immortal-shouldn't he slow down? Never one to bask in the glow and allow a sexy mood to be created, I decided to break it up. "Oh, you're just saying that to get into my pants," I teased.

Gregory looked at me for a moment and then burst out into his thick, rich laugh. "Now you've done it, Josie. Just for that comment, I refuse to sleep with you tonight." And that was okay, because just then I'd kinda managed to fuck myself pretty well.

After dinner I drove Gregory home. I walked him up to his door and he ran in and returned with my flowers, without asking me in for a nightcap.

"What, I don't get that nightcap?" I pouted a little.

"No, Josie, my feminist rose, you do not get that nightcap. I find myself smitten with you, dearest, and I don't want to ruin that by rushing things. Let me take you out on a date next. What do you think?"

"I would absolutely love that, Gregory, my molten vampire mystery. Name the night and I will be available."

We arranged for a date the next week and then we kissed.

Oh, it hurts to say it like that. "We kissed." So mundane. So average. So not the words I could use to describe the meeting of our mouths. We had kissed at the bowling alley and that was sweet and amazing, but the goodnight kiss was like nothing we'd done before. Gregory instigated the kiss. He bent his head down to mine and lightly pressed his lips to my forehead. I looked up at him and he came down and laid a butterfly kiss on the tip of my nose. He moved his head further and gently kissed each side of my jaw. It was like foreplay for the lip-locking part of the kiss. He finally slid up from my jaw to my lips with his lips slightly parted. He delicately pushed his tongue into my mouth and massaged my tongue with his. I matched the super slow, languid pace he set and it was the longest, deepest, slowest kiss ever. It wasn't frenzied like you might expect a kiss to be when two people are desperate to rip each other's clothes off, but it carried the same heat. It was so slow and so intense, I think I actually fainted in the middle of it from pleasure. I didn't even notice the giant bouquet of roses that I was holding getting crushed between us.

Eventually he lifted his face from mine. His eyes were dark and I could see him struggling with his desire. I could tell he was regretting forbidding me from sex tonight, and boy, so was I.

"Well, I should be getting back now," he said, still staring at me, lost in the desire and passion we'd found in the kiss.

"Um, Gregory?"

"Mmm, yes?"

"This is your house."

He looked behind him at the door and then back at me with his eyebrows drawn together as if he were confused. "Oh, yes, so it is. Then I guess you should be getting back now." He sounded even more distraught at that, although the outcome of either action would have resulted in the same physical separation.

"Yeah, yeah, I should. So Friday, right?"

He looked more hopeful then. "Oh yes, without a doubt. I'll be at your house at nine PM. Wear something comfortable."

"Comfortable as in...um...how comfortable?" I wasn't sure if we were even going to leave the house on our second date.

He chuckled and gently grabbed my chin between his thumb and index finger. As he lifted my face up for another kiss he murmured, "Clothes comfortable for walking in, and lingerie comfortable enough for lying down in."

CHAPTER 10

On Sunday morning, I was still replaying the highlights reel from my perfect date with Gregory when I remembered that I had a date with Walker later in the evening. I laughed to myself, thinking about how far from perfect it would likely be.

In contrast to the night before, I wasn't nervous at all prior to my date with Walker. I spent the day running errands and shopping and came home just in time to hop in the shower before the date.

Since we were only going to Rocket Burger and nowhere fancy, I decided to wear shorts and a tank top. I paired them with a pair of flip-flops. Not exactly dressed to impress, but definitely dressed to stand out in the heat looking at motorcycles and drinking beer.

As I was putting in some earrings I heard the distinct rumblings of an early model Ford barreling up the alley. I glanced out the window behind me through the reflection in my mirror and saw the most dusty, beat-up, ramshackle truck ever pull up to the curb in front of my house. I walked to the door and stepped out as Walker was ambling up my walkway.

He was dressed in typical Walker style, all black with a

long black trench coat over the ensemble just to keep things interesting. His dark blond hair was still sexily brushing his cheekbones and his green eyes seemed extra bright, possibly because they weren't hidden behind the haze of cigarette smoke.

"What are you, like Walker, Texas Ranger?" I asked. He looked at me, with confusion wrinkling his brow. "The four-wheel drive. We live in Florida, and not the swampy part. That's not the most practical vehicle for the area."

"What makes you think I live here?" he asked, his rough voice reinforcing the manly image set by his truck and his surly attitude. As he climbed up to my porch, I noticed that he had something in his hands. It looked suspiciously like a present.

"Oh, well, I guess I just assumed. Whatcha got there, Nicotine-o?"

"Just a little present. You can open it now or later tonight before I make love to you."

Okay, seriously, after he said that, you could have knocked me over with a feather. What did this obnoxious prick think? That I would just lean back and spread-eagle because he was a vampire?

Okay, so he kinda had a point there, but still, I only wanted to sex up the nice vampires. "Listen, Walker, you can just stop the foreplay now because we are not having sex tonight and we are certainly not making love."

He stared down at me with an annoyed look on his face. "I only said 'making love' because I thought that's how you girls liked to put it so you wouldn't feel like you were doing something wrong. Personally, I like to say screw."

"So I guess you're a romantic. Let's just get this over with, okay?"

"But you have to open your present first." He handed me a small box wrapped in bachelor wrapping paper; in other words, the Sunday comics.

I opened it up to find a little blue box. An infamous little blue box. A Tiffany's little blue box. My heartbeat accelerated quickly and I looked up at him and asked, "Okay, is there, like, a severed finger or something in here?"

"No, I ate that before I got here."

I jumped back from him and he snorted and shook his head. "Really, Josie, do you know anything at all about vampires? We don't eat severed body parts, you freak."

I turned my attention back to the present, which might or might not pull this badly started date out of the gutter, and opened it. Inside the tissue paper was a small silver mirror. It was small enough to fit in the palm of my hand and perfect for my purse.

"You bought this to replace the one I broke after the party?"

"I did. Don't break this one, it was much more expensive than the one you had."

At this point, I wasn't sure if Walker was passive aggressive, an asshole, or scared of intimacy, since he seemed to try to ruin every single sweet moment he created. I got on my tiptoes and planted a small kiss on his cheek.

"Thank you, Nicotine-o. I'll treasure it always." I turned to lock my door, then laced my arm into Walker's.

He raised his eyebrows at the contact. "What is this?" he asked, indicating my arm in his.

"Well, you seem to have some of the traits necessary to be a good date, but other parts of you are sorely lacking. I'm going to show you how to treat a lady."

"Well, those lessons will come in handy if I ever do decide to date a lady, but right now I'm seeing you so why bother?"

"Here's your first lesson, Walker. If you don't have anything nice to say, keep your mouth shut. Now, are we going to leave or what? I'm hungry for a burger and I need a beer like nobody's business."

"After you, m'lady." He bowed slightly and I led him to the truck, determined to salvage the evening.

CHAPTER 11

By the time we got to Rocket Burger, I felt like I'd been ridden hard and put away wet. And if I'd just been having sex that would have been great, but considering that I felt this way after a ten minute drive with Walker, it didn't bode well for the rest of the evening.

Walker, as a vampire, generally didn't get hot. So when the air conditioning went out in his truck, he saw no need to fix it. In order to keep me from suffocating or sweating *literally* to death on the ride to Rocket Burger, we had to drive with the windows rolled down. Naturally this didn't really cool me off so much as whip my hair into a crazy frenzy, get sand and road dust stuck to my face, and evenly spread my sweat all over my body. In short, I was disgusting.

We got out of the car and Walker asked me something, but I couldn't hear him over the roar of hundreds of motorcycles all revving their engines for bike night. Since I also can't read lips I simply looked at Walker stupidly, unsure how to even react to the sounds he was obviously trying to make.

"You have a hair," he shouted, "going up your nose!"

Of course I did. I ran my fingers through my hair and tried to make it look sexily tousled but I'm sure I didn't achieve the look. "Can we get a table?" I shouted back to him.

He smiled and grabbed my hand and then pulled me forward to the building. Rocket Burger is made up of two different sections. There is the original restaurant which is closed-in and air-conditioned and then there is the ramshackle shack portion of the restaurant which has a lovely and quaint dirt floor, picnic tables, and random two-by-fours with plywood crookedly affixed to them as "walls." How it has survived hurricane season in Florida for over fifty years is anybody's guess.

Walker led me to the unair-conditioned ramshackle portion of the restaurant and we sat down at an empty picnic table. Since my white shorts were already looking less than clean, I didn't bother to wipe off the seat. *To hell with it*, I thought. *It's not like we're going to be going on another date.*

The waitress came to our table and asked for our drink order. We both ordered beer and I went ahead and put in my hamburger order too. Walker, apparently, wasn't hungry because he didn't order anything in the way of food. Maybe I wasn't the only one that wanted to get this over with quickly.

I was surprised when Walker's hand reached across the table and rested on top of mine. One of my eyebrows went up and I looked at him. "Really? Is that really how you feel this date is going? It's going well enough to touch each other?"

He laughed. "I'm a man, Josie. We could be swinging bats at each other's heads and I'd still want to touch you."

Something about the way he said that made me ache a little for even more touching, and that ache disturbed me more than anything. I mean, Walker was an asshole. He was rude and insulting, didn't take anything seriously, he was an ass.

I pulled my hands off the table and rested them in my lap. "So tell me, Walker, what do you do for a living?"

He leaned back and pulled out a pack of cigarettes. Great. I was outside and stinky already and now I was going to have to suffer through cigarette smoke.

"I'm what you might call an independent consultant."

"Jesus, Walker, enough with the cryptic. You are an independent consultant or you aren't?"

"You might say that."

"Fuck me, you make it hard to like you, Nicotine-o."

"Now that's the best thing you've said all night." His lascivious smile told me that the "hard to like you" part of my sentence was not what he was referring to.

"Okay, Walker, here's the deal. You know me. You know my name, where I live, what kind of car I drive, where I work, what I do for a living. It's not like there's much left for you to find out about me. Can we just try to get on equal footing here? Can you give me at least one straight answer about yourself?"

Just then the waitress came back with our drinks and my food, which saved Walker from answering my question. As I ate, the band started setting up on the little stage in the corner.

"Do you like to dance?"

"Not really. I'm not very good at it," I answered between mouthfuls. What Rocket Burger lacked in tasteful ambience they made up for in tasty, beefy goodness.

"Really? I find that hard to believe. You walk like you'd be a good dancer."

"What the heck does that mean, Walker?"

He licked his lips and his lids dropped a little as though, if he squinted hard enough, he could see what I looked like naked. "You swing your ass when you walk. It's sexy and it usually means a girl's got rhythm."

"Walker, you really are a jerk. I almost feel bad for you, though, because I think it's a compulsion and you are actually helpless against it."

With a maddened glint in his eye, he leaned forward toward me and rasped, "You should punish me."

"Ha. Somehow I think your idea of punishment would be more punishing for me than it would you."

When the band started playing its first song, Walker suddenly grabbed my hands and looked at me with fire in his eyes. "Dance with me," he begged.

I was so caught off guard by his sudden intensity that I agreed. He pulled me up onto my feet and dragged me to the small area of dirt in front of the stage that was clear of tables and served as a pathetic makeshift dance floor, although it might actually have been just a sentimentally preserved relic of the dust bowl. Once we reached the dance floor he pulled me so tight against his body that I didn't need to make any movements of my own; I merely had to relax enough to let his body lead me.

As we swayed to some horrible hybrid heavy metal and country song, the smell of hot sauce, stale beer, and motor oil wafted through the air, which was humid and clung like Vaseline to my skin. It was a decidedly unsexy atmosphere. Walker bent down to bury his face in my neck…my dirty, sweaty neck which was currently itchy because my hair was stuck to it like seaweed to your legs at the beach. He rested his face in the crook of my neck and the feeling of his chilly breath against my skin overrode all my other senses until I felt cool and his breathing was the only atmosphere I noticed.

Then, suddenly, I began to feel very warm all over, despite the cool breeze coming from Walker's mouth or maybe because of it. His arms were pressed tightly around the small of my back and I could feel the length of his body against mine. I felt a warm, deep, guilty tug in my belly. My arousal was so sudden and intense that I didn't know if I wanted to weep, fuck, or yell out.

He whispered into my hair, "I want you." The gruff intimacy of his voice in my ear combined with the vibrations I felt being held against him as he spoke was like some sort of heady foreplay that almost made me forget who and where I was.

I pulled my head back enough to look at his face. I looked for any trace of mocking or some kind of horrible, ego shattering set-up and instead found that intense gaze. Like me, he almost looked pained from the physical reaction of our bodies touching.

"I just don't understand you, Walker. I don't know what to think about you." I searched his face for some clue to who he was, what his game was. I wanted so badly to give in to my body, but without some assurance that it wasn't a trap of some kind, I just couldn't feel comfortable letting go.

Suddenly, his green eyes got tight and went back to their usual wise-cracking glare and he laughed bitterly. "It's just sex, Josie. It's not like I'm proposing marriage."

I remained in his arms, feeling numb like I'd just been hit and felt the sting of tears in my eyes. Suddenly, the room came back to me and I was once again bathed in noisy, stinky, hot, and dirty air. I couldn't believe how close I'd gotten to trusting this asshole and making myself emotionally vulnerable to him.

The song ended and I wriggled out of his grip. Then I reached up and grabbed his chin, digging my nails into either side of his jaw, and pulled his face toward mine. "I want to make sure you hear me clearly, Walker. I never want to see you again. Stay away from me, away from my home, and away from my job, you asswipe. I'm not kidding. If I see you again I'll stab you in the fucking heart and I don't give a rat's ass about what your vampire enforcers say about it."

Walker looked surprised as I turned around and walked home.

CHAPTER 12

On Monday it was back to work as usual, though with a slightly bruised ego. When I got to work,

Megan told me there was a delivery for me on the front counter. She didn't seem very happy that I'd received a delivery at work so I assured her that I hadn't ordered anything. She rolled her eyes and said that would have been pathetic if I had, a comment that left me completely confused.

When I walked out from the employee area and looked toward the front counter I saw two huge arrangements of flowers taking up the entire counter space, and I realized what she meant. One vase was blood-red and filled with four dozen red, long-stemmed roses. They were perfect, if a bit antiseptic. I pulled the card out from the roses and found a note that said:

Miss you already.
Yours,
Gregory.

The second vase was clear glass and had blue irises with pink tulips. While it wasn't as impressive in size as the rose bouquet, the combination of flowers was breathtaking. I pulled the card out and found a note:

Forgive me?
Walker.

I moved both arrangements to the back of the shop and tried to focus on the work I had to do that day. It wasn't easy. I chatted up wedding parties and tried to pin gowns for alterations. I worked with brides to create their perfect bustle and consulted on the right length of tulle for veils.

However, the entire day all I could really focus on was how I felt about the flowers from Walker. Part of me, a really big, really horny part of me, wanted to forgive the ass. His split personality was weird, but I felt like there was something he wasn't telling me. Like, maybe he had some weird vampire disease and when he got hungry for blood he turned into a raging asshole and couldn't help himself.

I also started thinking about how perfect Gregory was. Something was nagging at my brain, as if his being perfect was a liability that I'd overlooked. But it bothered me that the minute I met a really nice guy who seemed totally into me, my mind had to wonder what was up with that. I mean, was I that much of a sadist? Would I never let myself be happy? After all, not every woman has to have an abusive, *Lifetime* movie type of relationship. Why couldn't I be the lucky one who got perfect Gregory?

I decided that the most logical next step was to call Alena and get an unbiased point of view. When I left work I loaded all my flowers into my car, then called her and asked her to meet me at my house. Since I was leaving work during rush hour, something I usually avoided because I worked in retail, the drive took me longer than usual, which really just gave me even more time to stew over the situation.

Alena had already let herself in when I got home and was sitting on the loveseat (the only thing that could fit in my cottage and serve the purpose of a sofa) pouring wine into two glasses, being careful not to let any splash on her perfectly white summer dress. Not for the last time, I was jealous of how her tanned skin and dark hair made white look like an exotic color. As a pale blonde, white just made me look like a Victorian ghost.

It wasn't often that she was able to get out of the house without the kids, so I asked her what she had to do to make this happen.

"Well, John and I didn't have any plans because he had a poker game tonight so I just brought the kids to their grandpa's house and told him either John or I would pick them up later. Now, tell me all about this vampire triangle you've trapped yourself into."

As I drank my wine I explained to Alena the situation and gave her an overview of each of the dates. "I don't know, Alena. The date with Gregory was much more romantic and smooth, but with Walker...God. For as much of an asshole as he is there are just these tremendous sparks between us. And, I feel like he isn't really as much of an asshole as he wants me to think he is."

"Josie, I don't get you. I know you've been going on and on about how you want to date a vampire. Well, now you've done yourself one better-you've dated two vampires. You've had that experience, now you can start looking for a real match. Someone to marry and have kids with. It's time to settle down, woman. Look at you, you're thirty-two and live in a one-room rental. Don't you want a house, children, and a career?"

I looked at Alena and thought about what she was saying. She and I had always been straight with each other so I wasn't exactly surprised by her illustrious dreams of my matrimonial future, but I was curious about how I felt about the image she was conjuring. As she mentioned each thing that she thought I should want to have-the house, the kids, the husband-I realized that I really didn't want those things. Not now, and maybe not ever. I enjoyed my life. I had fun. I did what I wanted and was accountable only to me. I didn't have to wait until the kids were at their grandparents' house and my husband was at a poker game before I could take time for myself. I didn't have a big house to clean and maintain, and my career brought me fun, variety, and social interaction. All in all, I was happy.

"I just realized something, Alena. I'm taking all of this too seriously. I don't have to choose anyone, give my heart away to anyone, or stop myself from seeing anyone. I simply have to do what I want to do. What seems fun and isn't harmful. And when something stops being fun, I don't have to do it anymore. I'm just really taking this too seriously. What's that saying? I'm putting the cart before the horse."

She was about to answer me when there was a knock on the door. I reluctantly got up from the love seat and opened the door to find Walker standing on my doorstep. He was wearing his usual ensemble of all black but he looked a little nervous. His green eyes were scanning my face, looking for something. And he smelled different. Instead of emitting a whiff of cigarettes, he smelled like a clean, spicy aftershave.

It was a yummy and somehow very male scent.

"Hi, Walker. What're you doing here?"

His words came out in a rush, like he didn't know where to begin. "Josie, did you get my flowers? I wanted to apologize. Can I come in?"

I felt bad for him, but I didn't know if I wanted to make this easy for him. "I have company right now, Walker, it's not a good time."

He looked instantly angry and put his hand on my arm as if to move me. "Is Gregory here?"

"No, it's not Gregory, but even if it were it wouldn't be any of your business. I got your flowers and your card. I can forgive you, Walker, I really can. I'm not sure what that really means for our relationship, but there you go."

He dropped his hand from my arm and looked at me. Then he grabbed my face and pulled me to him. He kissed me lightly on the lips, then more forcefully. He pried my lips apart with his mouth and plunged his tongue in to caress my own. His kiss had a frenzied pace, like the last kiss of a soldier about to be deployed. He must have recently eaten because his lips were scorchingly hot.

He took his hands from my face and slid them down to my waist, still holding me close to him. I lifted my arms to his neck and pulled my body against his. He moved his lips from my mouth down my neck and nibbled my earlobes. I sighed and my world narrowed to just the two of us until a throat cleared behind me and brought me back to reality.

Walker heard it too and stopped kissing me. "I'm going to go, but we need to talk. I'll be in touch." He kissed my forehead and then left.

I wrapped my arms around myself, trying to cling to the

warm feeling that Walker's visit had evoked as I stood at the door watching his truck leave. When I closed the door, I rested my head against it, unable to face Alena. I felt like I didn't want to be back in the real world yet. I didn't want to be out of that kiss yet. When I finally collected myself, I turned and saw Alena looking at me as though she'd never really seen me before.

"He's really hot, Josie."

"Yeah, he really is."

"Is the other one as hot?"

"Yup, he sure is."

"Neither one of them looks like an accountant," she said, though it seemed more for her own benefit than mine.

"What are you talking about, Alena?"

"John's friend-he's an accountant. He met you at one of our anniversary parties and wanted me to fix you up with him. When I came over today, that was what I'd planned to do. I thought it was time that you started taking your life seriously and looked for someone to settle down with."

"Yeah, I kinda got that from your earlier diatribe."

"Forget that, Josie. Let's pretend it never happened. You made me realize something today."

"What's that?"

"Sometimes settling down is just…settling."

PART 4 – SEX WITH VAMPIRES

The vampire reproductive system works like the human reproductive system with one major difference, the magic that is infused in vampires' blood that prevents them from dying a timely death and makes them unable to replace red blood cells also prevents their reproductive system from producing the eggs and sperm necessary for procreation. In addition, their blood also prevents venereal diseases from proliferating.

—Excerpt from a high school health book

CHAPTER 13

Friday came around and it was time for my second date with Gregory. I wore a pair of dark denim capris, a cute pair of sneakers with illustrated skulls covering their canvas, and a white tank top with a black short-sleeved button down top. I was showing just the right amount of firm but bouncy cleavage to ensure that Gregory would be equal parts proud of his arm candy and curious about its underlying details.

While waiting for Gregory I took a look at the paper. The usual killings, accidents, and political strife filled the pages. As I was flipping through pretending to read but really just trying to calm my second-date-potential-first-sex-tonight jitters, a picture caught my eye. At first, I thought there was a picture of me in the paper, but since I hadn't done anything newsworthy in, well, ever, I figured I was wrong and did a double take. Sure enough, there was a picture of a missing woman who was about my age and my size, with blonde curly hair. When I took the time to actually look at her, I realized that she didn't really look like me-just resembled me a bit.

A knock on the door told me that Gregory had shown up right on time, and the subsequent opening of the door showed me that he'd brought a gorgeous bouquet of roses with him. I took in the gloriousness that was Gregory, all dark hair, white teeth, deep tan, and eyes like sparkling coal, and briefly wondered if I hadn't underdressed just a bit.

Gregory was wearing a pair of dark dress pants and loafers with a dress shirt. He didn't have a tie on, but I still felt a little ill at ease with my choice of clothing. I invited him in and went into the kitchen to put the flowers in a vase. Actually, I had to put them in a beer stein because I didn't have any vases. When did I suddenly become that girl that guys sent flowers to? When I came out, Gregory was looking at my bookshelves.

"All ready to go?" he asked.

"Yuppers. Where are we going anyway?"

"We are going to a vampire picnic."

"What's a vampire picnic?" I asked, realizing that Gregory was probably overdressed. Maybe he hadn't been to a picnic before? We walked outside and I locked the door to my cottage as Gregory answered me.

"It's exactly what it sounds like, a picnic that vampires have. You might consider it a work event." I reached Gregory's Chrysler 300 and he held my door open for me, then walked around to the other side of the car. As he got in, he finished explaining the event. "We will be there with other enforcers and governors. It's just our way of reconnecting with each other, sharing stories and bonding," he said as he backed out of my driveway and headed toward the local park.

"You're taking me to a work event? Isn't that like making our relationship public?"

He glanced over at me. "Is that a bad thing, Josie?"

"No, no, it's…well…it's great, I just wasn't expecting it to happen so quickly. We haven't even…" I didn't really know how to end that statement without sounding…well…slutty.

"You know, that's very easy enough to rectify." He reached over and put his hand on my thigh. He slid it slowly down to my knee and then back up to my mid-thigh. I felt the familiar tug at the bottom of my stomach, and mentally patted myself on the back for wearing super cute undies. Then I remembered Walker's kiss a couple of nights earlier and my arousal quickly fled.

We pulled in to the park, and sure enough, there was a large picnic set up. Well, let me amend that. There was a banner announcing the picnic, although it was pretty hard to read at night, and there were a lot of vampires standing around with drinks in hand. The only thing really picnic-y about it were the picnic tables, and frankly, they came with the park so you can't really attribute their presence to any picnic vibe the vampires set.

I'd never been to a picnic at night before, and it was a bit unsettling. *Nightline* recently did a show debunking all the stupid vampire myths out there. They mentioned that vampires have a cellular deficiency (which is why they need to drink blood daily) and since free radicals caused by sun exposure can further ruin the cells that they've got, vampires have got to stay out of the sun. That means that most of their events are held at night. But a picnic at night is a strange experience. A chorus of cicadas took the place of chirping birds, and the normal accompaniment of barking dogs, laughing children, and bouncing balls were gone from the landscape. Instead, we were left with an empty, mumbly picnic.

"Josie, I'd like to introduce you to some people." Gregory pulled me from my reverie and, literally, grabbed my arm and brought me toward a group of waiting vampires.

"Madam Secretary, Governor Mullin, this is my lover, Josie."

Lover? What the…? Hold the phone-Gregory and I hadn't even had sex, much less become lovers. What was he doing? I didn't want to embarrass him in front of his work posse, but I made a mental note to ask him about this later.

I stretched out my hand to make nice with the vampire mucky-mucks but neither of them returned the favor. I was left with my hand out and pointed toward Madam Secretary. She sneered down at my wavering appendage and rested both of hers on the cup she had, as though the burden of holding a cup was reason enough to not touch me. She nodded her head and then began speaking to Gregory with a friendly smile. I turned myself at the waist so that my hand was pointing to the gentleman Gregory introduced me to and got the same sneer, but he wasn't even polite enough to grab onto his cup. He simply ignored me.

I stood there feeling like a third wheel on a unicycle, catching snippets of conversation not at all directed at me. Gregory threaded his arm through mine, held me close to his side, and kissed the top of my head mid-conversation. I could only assume that this meant he was not surprised or put off by their reaction to me, which was nice.

I used this opportunity to look around the park. None of the vampires were dressed as casually as I was. It seemed like picnic translated into cocktail party to these formal people, as I might have expected when I saw how Gregory was dressed. I would normally have been put off by this, but if everyone was going to be needlessly rude to me I figured they could just suck it and deal with my sardonic skeletal footwear.

Gregory finished his conversation with the snoots and we began to walk away. A column of black to my left caused my heart to thud unreasonably and I sucked in my breath as I thought I saw Walker coming toward us. But it must have been wishful thinking because it was just a garbage can. I made yet another mental note, this time to let Walker know I had mistaken a garbage can for him, and then I realized I could be up for a big case of awkward if we ran into him tonight. I added this issue to my list of "Things to resolve with Gregory post-haste" and decided to get started.

"Um, Gregory, why did you introduce me as your...uh, lover?" I looked at him from under my lashes, too embarrassed to make real eye contact.

He chuckled and leaned his cheek on the top of my head. "Ah, Josie. I realize I jumped the gun, but only by a few hours, right?"

I wasn't sure if I should be annoyed at the lack of seduction in his presumptuous mention of our future lovemaking or just be super excited that I was finally going to have hot, not-very-sweaty vampire sex. I opted for the latter.

"Oh, yeah, true," I said breathlessly as I contemplated our coupling.

Gregory stopped walking and removed his arm from mine, then turned to face me. He put his hands on either side of my arms and pulled me in for a kiss. We were in public, so he couldn't go sloppy sexy, but he went with buttoned-up and neat sexy. He ran his tongue along mine slowly and built up the prickly burn I'd felt earlier in the car. As he stoked my lust, it grew and broadened deep into my breasts, down my legs, and into my back. Before that moment, I hadn't even known you could feel lust in your back but, uh, yeah, you can.

We disengaged, rethreaded our arms, and began walking as I tried to regain my composure. We were headed toward a group of vampires and I had the sudden fear that we might run into Walker and that could ruin any chance at sex I had later. To be honest, thoughts of Walker brought in some weird sexual tension of their own and I found myself confused again over my feelings for each of these men. But no matter what century they came from, we were in the twenty-first, and that meant that I could date two men as I figured out which one was the better fit. And sleeping with them, as far as I was concerned, needed to be part of that process.

I decided to bring Walker up now, just in case. "Hey, is Walker going to be here tonight?" I realized as I said it that this was not the vampire's real name, but the name he'd told me to call him.

Gregory looked as though he was considering this. "Walker…I don't recall a Walker. Is this someone you met at my party?"

"Yeah. Well, no. Okay, sort of. He was outside smoking when I left your party."

Gregory stopped before I realized he was going to, which resulted in me continuing to walk a bit and feeling as though my arm was going to be pulled out of its socket since it was connected to the super-strong not walking vampire.

Something between a hiss and a growl erupted from Gregory's throat and he pulled me back, leaned into me, and urged, "Describe him."

"Well, he's tall. I guess your height. Thinner or, no, more narrow than you. Dark blond hair, wears all black. Kinda surly."

"Josie, was he in my condo?"

"I don't know. I mean, I didn't see him inside, I saw him outside, like I said. But come to think of it, he did tell me later that he'd spoken to you about me at the party."

"Later? You've seen him since the party?" If Gregory had been holding a cup of water at that moment, I think it would have boiled. His voice was tight and choked and he was squeezing my arm hard. Too hard.

"Yeah, a few times. Look, Gregory, can you let go of my arm while we discuss this? You're obviously upset but you're kinda hurting me."

He looked at me for what seemed a long time with a tightness in his eyes. Then an easiness washed over his face and his almost black eyes started to sparkle again. He loosened his hold on my arm and chuckled.

"I'm sorry, darling, I didn't mean to hurt you. I forget my own strength sometimes. The man you are talking about, he was once a close friend of mine but we've had a falling out recently. It's really nothing, but when you're friends as long as we've been you get emotionally attached. I overreacted."

"Oh...'kay. So, is he going to be here tonight?"

"No, Josie, this picnic is just for enforcers and governors. The man you call Walker is not in that group. He is more of a rogue character. Really, he is not someone you should be associating with. Obviously it's not my place to tell you whom you should or should not develop a friendship with, but I'm afraid this Walker is a danger to you."

I was surprised to feel my stomach fall when Gregory

said that. I trusted his judgment; after all, he'd known Walker for years and I'd known him just a few days-but I guess some part of me really wanted to believe that somewhere, deep...*deep* down inside, Walker was good. I wanted to ask Gregory more about him and what he'd done, but we finally reached the next crowd of vampires.

Once again, Gregory introduced me and once again, the vampires not only refused to shake my hand but also managed to make me feel like my fingers were full of slime and drool. If I had a nickel for every sneer I received in lieu of a smile, I'd be able to invest in some designer footwear.

Most of the night continued in the same way, with me being sneered at and Gregory being happily received. Occasionally, I caught a whiff of stale cigarettes and each time I did I felt excitement filling my chest, but as I looked around I never actually saw...uh...anyone smoking. It wasn't until we were getting ready to leave that a vampire at the picnic actually stopped to acknowledge my capacity for conversation and stooped from his super high pedestal to talk to me.

We had approached the last table in the park and there was a group of three vampires standing in front of it. One of them was a brunet male of average height with a buzz cut that made him look like a hot soldier. To his right was a tall blonde female vampire with legs that seemed to go all the way to her neck. Next to her was a short, young vampire with red hair and a charismatic smile. Now, when I say young I mean that he had probably been turned in his late twenties. How long ago that was I had no idea. It struck me that, had he not been turned, he would have grown into one of those kindly old gentlemen with an ever-burning pipe and welcoming twinkle in his eye. Gregory introduced me to all of the vampires and I learned that the redhead's name was Governor Thurston Harnett.

Governor Harnett was the only vamp who lowered himself to address me. "Josie, what a pretty name. Is it short for something?"

A lot of people thought my name was short for something. "Nope, just Josie."

"So, how did you meet our favorite enforcer, Gregory?"

"He had a party a couple of weeks ago and I happened to be there. The rest, as they say, is history." I don't think the last part made any sense, but I'd wanted to use that phrase forever and thought there was no time like the present.

"Mmmm, yes, so they say. And what are your plans for our Mr. Bullster?"

"Tonight or over the long-term?" I asked, looking him dead in the eye.

He paused for a moment as if evaluating me, and then chuckled reluctantly. "That was a good retort, young lady. Maybe you can handle a vampire relationship after all."

After that, Thurston seemed to warm to me. He asked about my work and hobbies and we exchanged a few jokes. We even had some music preferences in common.

Gregory eventually turned from the conversation he was having with the tall female vampire who was introduced as Governor Wartham and who had a face like a squished lemon. He turned to Thurston and me and joined our little tête-à-tête.

"Thurston, tell me that you haven't revealed all my darkest secrets to sweet Josie so that she'll run away with you?"

"Hardly, Gregory. And even if I had, something tells me

she wouldn't necessarily run away from you. She's a fine, strong girl." It seemed weird to have a guy who looked younger than me talk about me the same way my grandfather might talk about me...or a farm animal.

"I agree, Thurston. Well, Josie and I have other plans this evening, so I think we'll take our leave."

"Of course. It was wonderful to meet you, Josie. Are you going to take her to your warehouse, Gregory? I understand you have some things in storage that are of interest to many people."

Gregory stood stock-still, and seemed to be debating how he was going to answer that question. "Yes, I believe I will at some point, Thurston, but not this evening. We have other plans that don't involve looking at dusty relics from my former life."

CHAPTER 14

On the drive back to Gregory's condo, he filled me in on all the gossip about everyone we met at the party. I really didn't give a rat's ass about anyone except Thurston.

"I've known Thurston since the fifteen hundreds. He was a tailor in London and was often called upon to create new suits for King Henry the Eighth's court."

"Wait-THE King Henry the Eighth? Oh. My. God. Did he really have syphilis and throw food on the floor?"

"Josie, don't be absurd. First of all, banquets were much different then. I'm sure there were times that food was 'thrown on the floor,' but I would certainly hope that's not all that King Henry is known for. Secondly, I'd rather not talk about festering sex wounds tonight of all nights."

"Oh, yeah, good idea. So how did you two meet?"

"Well, we met just after he'd been turned. Of course, vampires were not a known entity then, so he was trying to blend in as a human and still run his shop. He'd been called many times to court to do some tailoring during the day but as a new vampire, he was sleeping much of that time and unable to make the journey out-even if he had the use of a protective vehicle. Eventually, Henry took offense. He thought Thurston was being obstinate and ordered him to be beheaded."

"What? That's crazy. Then what happened?"

"Well, Thurston had heard about me through the grapevine and asked me to help him leave his old life and begin anew. I smuggled him out of the country and got him started in Germany with a new name, new identity, and new business."

"Is that what you were? A smuggler?"

"I have been many things, Josie. It wasn't always easy for vampires to make a living. At the time, I did some human and other smuggling."

We were quiet for a moment, and I realized that I didn't know the story of how Gregory had been turned into a vampire. "Is it too personal for me to ask how you became a vampire?"

"It is sometimes traumatic for a vampire to recount his or her story. In my case, it is not since it was something I asked for."

"So you knew about vampires and actually asked to become one?"

"I did. There was a time when I thought knights were the most powerful men besides kings-obviously, this was before I learned about vampires. For years I wanted nothing more than to be an honorable, strong, and powerful knight. Unfortunately, I was not in line to become a knight, so I joined the church and became a monk. I felt that bringing peace and God's love to pilgrims was a different kind of power that, while not equal to knighthood, would do."

"So how were you turned?"

"I had taken to walking in the evenings before bed. One

night, I was heading back to the monastery after a stroll when I came upon a man standing in the path. He was standing still, just looking at me as I headed toward him. I thought he might need aid. People were always traveling to the monastery looking for work or assistance of some kind, so I approached and asked what he was doing there. He looked past me as though waiting for someone else and said, 'Proceed on, monk. I wait for company other than yours.' I searched his face and while I could find no outward signs of anything unique about him, I knew he was...different. At the time, I thought maybe he was touched by God and I remained standing there, in awe of him. He again urged me on, saying, 'You may remain, monk, but you will not like what you see, and do not think to stop me.' Soon, I heard the sound of a carriage and realized that another traveler was, in fact, heading our way.

"This new traveler saw us both in the path and must have felt some ill will coming from the mysterious man, because he tried to speed up and go around us. But his carriage could not navigate the bumpy trail and it tipped as he tried to go around. The man who had been standing in the road jumped on top of the overturned carriage and began feasting on the older gentleman who had been driving. He lifted the man's body as though it weighed nothing more than a sack of potatoes, he was so strong. All of my earlier dreams of power, strength, and knighthood came back to me and soon, the thought of serving God was very far from my heart and just as I'd once longed for knighthood, I now wanted what this man had."

"So you asked him what he was and then asked him to turn you?"

"Yes."

"And it didn't bother you that, in order to have this strength, you would have to kill people and drink their blood?"

"Well, we didn't know then that it wasn't necessary to kill people in order to survive, but yes, I was willing. As a vampire, I was able to make sure that I didn't kill women or innocent men, and I never hurt children, so I felt that my code as a vampire was as chivalrous as a knight's."

"But…what did you think about what God would think about you becoming a vampire?"

Gregory took his eyes from the road for a brief moment and gave me a sidelong glance. "I didn't know where to fit my concept of God into my new life as a vampire. Hell, I didn't know where to fit God into my life the moment I realized the man I met in the road was a vampire."

We sat in a comfortable, if contemplative silence as we drove the rest of the way. Eventually we pulled up to Gregory's building and he opened my door for me. I slid out of the car and felt a little uncomfortable. Our conversation in the car hadn't really lent itself to foreplay, and I wasn't really sure what we were going to do next.

"Josie, would you like a nightcap?" As he asked me, Gregory grabbed my hand and brought it to his lips, never once breaking eye contact with me. His eyes were like deep whirlpools. Once again, I felt my lusty pot simmer and decided that upstairs was exactly where I wanted to be.

I nodded my head and Gregory slipped his arm around my waist and led me up to his condo.

Once inside he turned on the lights and put on some soft music. "What would you like to drink?"

"Whatever's easy." Shit. Now I was concerned that I had Freudian slipped the thought of me being easy into Gregory's mind. Maybe this really wasn't a good idea after all.

"Champagne?" He walked into the living room area while I was looking at his music collection. He had a chilled bottle of champagne, two glasses, and a vase with a single rose on a tray. "Josie," he said as he set the tray down and patted the seat on the settee next to him, "come."

This kinda made me feel like he was calling me as he would a cute little Pomeranian, but I didn't generally get a male chauvinist pig vibe from Gregory so I decided that I was being overly sensitive.

I sat next to him and he handed me a champagne flute.

He raised his glass toward mine and said, "To the future. May it be bright and full of happiness and fulfillment." We clinked glasses and drank.

Gregory set his glass down and rested a hand on my knee. "You know, Josie, we don't have to do anything tonight. Why don't we just sit, enjoy the music and champagne, and talk?"

My shoulders relaxed immediately and I felt myself sink into his cozy couch. He leaned in to me and put his left arm around my shoulders. He reached his right arm over his chest and played with my curls. "Tell me about your secret desires, Josie. What do you want to be when you grow up?" His voice was husky and full and I felt lulled into a place of trust and relaxation.

"Gosh, I don't really know. I'm not a real big planner. I just sort of roll with the punches. I like working with brides and might try to break out into consultancy someday." While I'd been talking, Gregory had taken his right arm and begun stroking my arm, face, and neck slowly.

"A consultant? Would you help the brides plan their entire event then?"

"Yeah, sort of like a wedding planner, but I want to work in more of a consulting capacity. Guiding them and giving them advice and solutions, but not really arranging everything." It was becoming harder and harder for me to concentrate as Gregory's caresses became more distracting and enjoyable. With every stroke of his hand it felt as though he were urging my desire to reach out to another part of my body and inflame it.

He must have felt my heartbeat accelerating because he suddenly took my face in his hands and turned it toward him, then lowered his mouth to mine.

Our lips met with a soft but crushing pressure. I turned more of my body toward Gregory and laced my hands around his head. I ran my fingers through his thick hair as he pushed his tongue through my lips to stroke mine. His mouth worked its way down my face to nuzzle my neck and his tongue reached out to lick the super sensitive area behind my earlobe.

I moaned as he probed his tongue around all my most erogenous zones-earlobes, jaw, neck, and those little indentations on the base of my neck above my collarbone. The pace of our kissing sped up and became more urgent as my hands glided over his chest and felt his hard body beneath my trembling fingers.

He groaned loudly as I ran my tongue down his neck and did a little ear play of my own. Before I realized what was happening, he'd put his right arm under my knees and his left around my back and he carried me to the bedroom.

He laid me on the bed gently, as if I were made of glass, then crawled onto the bed and over to me. As he moved toward me he began to remove his shirt. To level the playing field, I took off my black shirt and slipped the tank top over my head in one easy movement.

We were both on his bed, him without a shirt, me in just a bra, and his eyes rested on my breasts. He looked like a twelve-year-old who had just gotten the keys to a candy store while the owner was on vacation. He lowered his mouth to the mounds of flesh straining against their super pretty bra-shaped cage and, like a kid with some ever-lasting Gobstoppers, went in for a taste.

He began to lick the top of my right breast and then, slowly, he slipped his tongue underneath the bra. It was a tight fit, and something about the wet, single-minded determination of his tongue combined with the constricted bra made me lift my hips and cry out with pleasure as he finally flicked my hardened nipple with the tip of his tongue.

My cry made Gregory even more excited and his breathing sped up. He eased my bra off and started licking my left nipple as he ran his thumb over my right. I brought my hands down to his groin and felt him straining against the front of his pants. I slowly rubbed his shaft through his pants, moving my hands up and down. His muffled cry vibrated against my breast, bringing new levels of arousal to my body.

I undid his belt, then his pants, and he paused his breast play in order to help me remove his clothes. Eventually, he was positioned before me totally nude and totally ready. My breath caught in my throat as I looked him over. I had never been with a more physically perfect man. Never. His body was as perfect as a marble statue but in soft, pliable flesh.

He crawled back up the bed with a predatory look in his eyes and unbuttoned my capris with his teeth, lips, and tongue. As he did, he ran his tongue along my stomach and nipped my skin in a decidedly predatory manner. He yanked my pants over my hips and down my legs until they ended up in a pile on the floor. Then he began to run his tongue over my clit through my underwear.

He moved to the seam of my underwear along my inner thighs. He licked the skin running alongside the seam until I thought I'd scream in frustration. He used his nose to push my underwear to the side and placed his tongue on the skin of my burning hot center. I screamed out and pulled his hair and Gregory growled as he realized his super slutty date didn't need any more foreplay.

He slid my panties down my legs and eased his body up over mine until the tip of his shaft was poised outside my opening. He moved up and down and teased my entry. Then he rubbed the tip of his length around my clit, bringing me to the brink of complete satisfaction. He slowed his pace and my breathing became savage and ragged with need while my face gained a wild, frenzied look like a captured animal who never knew if it would be free again.

My eyes met his and as he saw my urgency, they became wolf-like again. He smiled and then shoved his length into me quickly and hard. No more easing, teasing, or toying with it. He entered me fully in one quick shot.

He positioned his hips so that every stroke rubbed my clit and my hips tried to match his rhythm. Between the friction and the rubbing, I came. The orgasm happened so quickly that I didn't even have time to warn Gregory that it was about to happen.

As my pleasure rippled through and squeezed his length, he buried his face in my neck and growled as he too reached fulfillment. It seemed to go on forever and take up my entire world for hours. Eventually, we both stopped and Gregory lay next to me as I nestled my head on his shoulder.

After I recovered my breath, I realized that he hadn't bitten me during sex. *Great*, I thought, *time to let the awkward post-initial-coitus apologies begin.* "I forgot to give you permission to bite me during sex. I'm sorry. I hope it didn't ruin it for you."

He was quiet for so long that I thought I must've really screwed up this vampire sex thing. I looked up at him and he had the most puzzled expression on his face.

"Tell me, Josie, would that have been better for you if you'd eaten a salami sandwich while we did it?"

"Ew, no. What an absurd question…oh. So then, you don't like to suck blood while you have sex?"

"No, Josie, I do not. Blood is for replenishing my body, not for sex."

"But, in all the books and on the movies, vampires always have a very sexual bite."

"This is true. Also, in books and movies, humans rarely use the restroom and the heroines in almost all vampire romance novels are almost never over twenty-nine. What is your point?"

I guess my point was that I was extremely gullible. Truth is, I never really took the time to try and actually get to know a vampire, I was just so single-mindedly obsessed with having sex with them.

Oh my God-I was a teenage boy.

CHAPTER 15

After a good night's sleep in Gregory's comfortable bed, and the strange feeling that always accompanies the first night spent with a new beau, I woke with an epiphany on my mind and a burning hunger in my tummy. I realized what a self-absorbed, single-minded nitwit I had been and decided to endeavor to know Gregory better. I also endeavored to use bigger, more adult words, like…endeavored.

I rolled over to face Gregory and was shocked to see him awake and looking back at me. Time for some smooth, Look at me, I'm taking time to get to know you now talk. "So tell me more about yourself, Gregory." As soon as the words were out of my mouth I realized that this was probably the worst sentence to ever say to someone you'd just had sex with and slept next to. I mean, it sounded like we were at a tea party for fuck's sake. So I followed up with more. "I know that you are an enforcer, what do you have to do as one?"

He rubbed my shoulder gently and cleared his throat. "Well, as an enforcer I mete out punishment to vampires who have committed crimes against humanity or their vampire brethren."

"I don't really understand what you're saying. Like, you put them in vampire jail?"

"Sometimes, it just depends on the sentence that the governors want executed. If they say jail, then we have a specialized holding facility that I must transport them to. Sometimes, the punishment is worse than that, and when it is, I must-for lack of a better word-execute it as well."

I felt like I understood what he was trying to get at but decided that I needed to hear more. "What would be a worse punishment than vampire jail?"

He sat up and looked at me, as if considering whether or not I could handle his news. He had a serious look in his eyes.

"Death, Josie. Death would be worse than that."

I frowned, wondering how I could balance my view of Gregory as a sweet, considerate man (and fanfuckingtastic lover) with that of Gregory the Enforcer, murdering vampires. As I considered this I realized that it might not matter much what I thought about it, but I wanted to hear what Gregory felt about it.

"Does it bother you to kill other vampires, Gregory?"

He absently rubbed his chin and looked off into space. "Not really. Not if they deserve it, that is. I don't think I would enjoy a cold-blooded killing, however."

For some reason, that made me feel better. I mean, after all, it's not like humans don't have their own death sentences and I would never hate the guy who had to administer the lethal injection that ended some person's life, although I might wonder what kind of person could do that and still sleep at night.

But then, why didn't I feel that way about Gregory?

Thinking about how to broach that question, I started with the logistics. "So do you give them some sort of lethal injection or something?"

Gregory turned his head down to look at me and something slipped over his eyes, something harsh and angry. "Why are you asking me these questions, Josie?"

He leaned down toward me with his face getting uncomfortably close to mine and he growled, "Planning something, are you, Josie?" As his words hit me like a verbal fist, his hand squeezed my shoulder way too hard.

I scooted away from Gregory, disengaging my shoulder from his hand, and hopped indelicately out of bed to start putting my clothes on. "Uh, yeah, planning to put my clothes on and get out of weirdsville, Gregory. Jesus, I was just curious. Humans have lethal injection as the death penalty manner of punishment and I wondered if vampires did the same. What the fuck is wrong with you?"

He looked at me from the bed, still with the hazy fog of anger over his eyes. "Perhaps it's time you went home, Josie."

"Uh, yeah, tell me something I haven't managed to figure out on my own, fucktard. I think you bruised my shoulder, you ass."

He seemed completely nonplussed by the physical pain he caused me, to say nothing of the emotional confusion, and just focused on getting me out of there. "I'll call a car for you."

"Forget it, Gregory, I'll just call myself a cab." I grabbed my purse and stormed out of his condo and went outside to call a cab.

CHAPTER 16

The cab smelled like it'd been slept in by ten retired circus clowns who'd gotten jobs scooping horse poo with their hands. I was so upset about what happened between Gregory and me that I didn't even bother to care that I was steeping myself in Eau de Poopie Clown.

I paid the driver and hopped out once we'd reached my house. I got my keys out and headed up the walkway to the front door. I positioned my key to go in the lock and found the door cracked open and the doorknob completely torn off and resting on the floor of my porch.

"Jesus, seriously? Now? Right now someone has to break in?"

I pushed the door with my foot and then stepped back to assess the situation. The crime rate in my neighborhood was next to nothing, but I'd obviously been a victim...unless the wind tore my doorknob off the door and left it ajar. And that was about as likely as pigs flying from any of my orifices. For a second, the image of the missing woman flashed in my mind and I wondered briefly if my night of passion had helped me avoid being the next victim.

I didn't see anything as I looked into the room from the

porch so I decided to tempt fate and go in. I grabbed my Mace out of my purse and held it in front of me like a gun, bending my knees and waist to obtain a sort of crouching position that kept my ass as far from the scene as possible. I don't know why this is the popular posture for people with guns, but it has been since I was a little girl watching *Charlie's Angels*, so I figured keeping your ass out of the way of impending doom must be paramount to survival.

I stepped over the threshold and scanned the room. The curtains were drawn, which was not how I had left them the night before. I was wondering what kind of anal burglar would bother with my curtains when a pile of black clothing with a man inside of it caught my eye. I sucked in my breath and backed into the wall, not at all something you do to defend yourself, and my Mace hand began to shake. Then I smelled cigarettes.

"For fuck's sake, you are disgusting. Please tell me you are not smoking in my home," I said to Walker as my adrenaline and fear-filled eyes started to make out details again and recognized the man in black who was reclining on my bed.

"I hope you haven't popped the safety on that deadly bottle of Mace in your hands."

"Jesus, Walker, do not start. You owe me some sort of explanation as well as a new door."

He sat up in the bed and for the first time I really took in his face. His normally clean-shaven chin had stubble dotting its landscape and his green eyes were pinched and worried looking. "Where have you been?"

"What do you...wait, Walker, are you really going to break into my home and then start Twenty Questions as though I'm the one who's done something wrong?"

Faster than I could follow, Walker rose from the bed and came to stand before me. He put his hand on the hand that held the Mace and pushed it down. His other hand stroked my face and his eyes searched me as if looking for some evidence of damage or mistreatment.

After the morning I'd had with Gregory, I actually did have some damage but not anywhere Walker would be able to see it-unless vampires had X-ray vision and he could see my heart and my pride.

"I'm sorry, Josie. I came over last night when I saw you and Gregory leave the picnic. I waited outside for you but you never came home."

Somehow, although it was none of his business what I did with my time, Walker was making me feel guilty, as if I should have been here for him. And that was really pissing me off.

"Walker, why don't you call next time before you come over? Because, you know, that's what most people do. They say to themselves, 'Self, I think I'll visit so-and-so today. But I'll call them first to make sure it's a good time.' That would be so cool if you would try something like that because I'm sure as hell not buying a new door every time your ass decides it wants to come over here when I'm away."

Suddenly, he reached into his pocket and pulled out a slightly crumpled sheet of paper with a picture on it and shoved it in my face. "Have you seen this?" he asked.

I grabbed at the picture and tried to slide along the wall to give myself some room, but he wasn't having any of it and he trapped me by putting his hands against the wall on either side of my face. I uncrumpled the paper and saw a picture of the same woman I'd seen in the newspaper the day before along with some information about how tall she was and where she was last seen. "Yeah, this is the woman who was in the paper yesterday. She's missing, right?"

"Look at the date on that sheet of paper, Josie."

I glanced down and saw that this missing persons flyer had been printed a week ago. I felt my face distorting in confusion. "They waited a week to write an article in the paper about her being missing?"

"No, Josie-this is a different woman. Can you tell me why that is interesting?"

"But she…she looks so much like the other one and…"

"And what, Josie? And she looks like you? Well, she's missing that charmingly confused look in her eyes but still, the resemblance is definitely there."

I stared at the picture and tried to understand what he was saying. He reached out to touch my face again, then dropped his hand and stared at me, squinting his eyes as though trying to see inside my brain. Finally, he gave up and walked over to my bed. He sat down on the side of it and put his face in his hands. "Josie, I don't know what's happening to me."

He sounded like he was about to cry and I was totally confused. I dropped the paper on the floor, walked over to the bed, and sat next to him, my hips and knees gently brushing the side of his body. "What's wrong, Walker? Tell me what's going on."

He lifted his head and turned to me and the confusion in his eyes was overwhelming. I didn't know why he had been living in turmoil, but I knew that he had been.

"Tell me first where you've been."

"Walker, why do we have to play some kind of weird verbal chess every time we see each other? You know exactly where I've been and, for that matter, can probably guess exactly what I've been doing."

He reached over and squeezed my hand. "I need to hear you say it. I need you to hurt me."

"I was...with Gregory last night."

He squeezed my hand even as his eyes glazed over with something like shock and I smelled something burning. "Walker, one of your nasty cigarettes is burning my bed."

He didn't look away and didn't even bother to move his cigarette from my comforter. "Well, isn't that symbolic?" he said. "Last night you were burning up the bed of an asshole and here I am, dying to explore your body and let the heat of our passion burn your sheets, but only able to burn your bed with a cigarette." He let out a short, barking laugh, let go of my hand, stood up, and began to pace.

Since he was obviously not going to deal with the cigarette, I reached over and lifted it off the bed and carried it to the toilet. As I did this he paced back and forth.

"Walker, you're going to wear a hole in my floor if you keep going like that. Talk to me and tell me what is bothering you. Is this because I slept with Gregory? You knew I was seeing him and this is the twenty-first century, you know-women can have sex before marriage now, with many different men even, and not be considered damaged goods."

But Walker wouldn't stop pacing. He seemed to be working his way up to saying something but I had no idea what it could possibly be. I decided to just pretend he wasn't there. I wanted to take a shower and wash off the last vestiges of the supremely conflicted and assholish Gregory.

"Walker, I'm going to take a shower. I'm guessing I'm

stuck with you for the day since you can't leave here until nightfall. Make yourself comfortable on the loveseat. I hope you've already eaten because I don't have any blood here. "

Moving as quickly as Gregory had this morning, Walker was suddenly in front of me with a crazy look in his eyes. He grabbed my shoulders tightly, but without hurting me, and I watched as his fangs extended.

"Oh, I don't know, Josie, I wouldn't say there's no blood here at all, would you? Or wait, did you give all of that to Gregory too?"

After everything Walker had put me through and the way he had treated me over the past week, I still didn't think he was going to attack me and steal my blood. "Walker, what are you doing? I may not know you that well, but this isn't you. You don't go around threatening to steal people's blood. What is the deal?"

The crazy left his face and his shoulder grab turned into a hug as he cried out in my neck, "You don't even know me, Josie, and yet, it's like you know me better than anyone ever has. How do you do that? How do you see through to my soul so easily?"

He pulled his head back to look at me searchingly and before I could respond he kissed me hard. His kiss had the same urgency I'd felt at Rocket Burger. As he took greedily from my mouth he backed me toward the bed until I was lying down and he was on top of me.

"Wait, Walker, no. I need…I need some time. I'm so confused right now."

"Josie, I want Gregory off of you. I want to take his scent, his hands, his influence away from you. Come."

He reached out his hand to me and I took it as he led me

to the bathroom. It did not escape my notice that he was the second vampire in a twenty-four-hour period to talk to me like I was a Pomeranian rather than a person.

When we got into the bathroom he plugged the tub and began filling it with warm water. He turned to me and began undressing me. "Um, Walker, I usually take off my own clothes, you know."

He was unbuttoning my shirt and he met my eyes with a pained look. "Please, Josie, just please let me do this."

I got the sense that this was part of some sort of important ritual for Walker. Like a baptism or something, but it was through the cleansing of my body that our relationship could be born again. As I looked at his eyes and his face, I physically hurt for him. So much so that I forgot about my own pain and fight with Gregory earlier. "Okay, Walker," I said gently, "just tell me what you need me to do."

After removing all my clothes, I was left standing in my bra and undies. Walker had been gentle and purposeful when removing my clothes, and he looked greedily at me while I stood in my bra and panties, but he also looked pained.

"Okay, Walker, what's next? What do you need?"

"The underwear. You wore that for him?" He looked in my eyes with such a mixture of pain and anger I literally ached for him.

"Yes, Walker, I did," I said quietly.

"Take it off," he pleaded with his voice and his eyes.

I slowly moved my hands back to disconnect my bra and pulled the straps down my arms. Once it was removed, I dropped the bra on the floor and then dropped my underwear and stood there, naked as the day I was born.

Walker stood staring at me as if he wanted to meld our

bodies together somehow and make me as much a part of him as his arms or legs were. He knelt and picked up my bra, ripped it up into tiny pieces, and threw it into the trash can.

Then he stood in front of me and lifted me to bring me to the bathtub. He set me in the warm water and knelt by the side of the tub. He reached for a washcloth and the soap and started sudsing up his hands.

He ran his hands and the bar of soap over every inch of my arms, stomach, back, and legs. As he did, his coat sleeves got drenched, but he didn't seem to notice. He left my more personal regions alone and nodded to indicate I should go ahead with those areas. Then he washed off the soap with the washcloth. He was methodical and deliberate, but it wasn't sexual or seductive. It was cathartic and relaxing and made me feel as though I were being given a fresh start at life.

When he was done and I was clean, he lifted me into a standing position and placed the towel around my torso, drained the bathtub, and carried me to bed. Once there he removed his coat and shirt, lay down, and wrapped himself around me.

CHAPTER 17

The man who called himself Walker held me all day as I slept. The entire day I was assaulted by dreams of cast-off women, used for sex and then thrown aside like yesterday's garbage. It's not like I hadn't gone through that before. These days, almost every unattached woman over thirty has felt the sting of a man who was only interested in her so far as it took to get her to have sex with him. So it wasn't Gregory's seeming dismissal that hurt so bad, it was my own gullibility in thinking we might be starting a relationship, not just having a fling. It was almost as though dating a vampire had reversed my relationship maturity and put me back to my gullible twenties, not a place I wanted to visit again. And while I'd given in to Walker's comfort after Gregory's dismissal, I wasn't blind to the fact that he, too, made me feel like I was brand new to the dating scene rather than a seasoned woman.

I woke to the feeling of Walker gently running his fingers along my shoulder and I stiffened. I rolled onto my back and sat up, looking down at him. "Evening, cowboy, looks dark outside. Guess that means your forced imprisonment is over." I bent my head toward the door, which Walker had barricaded with my loveseat sometime during the day.

Walker rolled onto his back and looked up at me. "Is that what you think this was? Forced company? I'm the one who broke into your house, Josie. Believe me, I wasn't forced to stay anywhere."

I sighed and got out of bed. I put on some jeans and a T-shirt from the dresser and tried to remove the loveseat from my door. "You should go, Walker. You can have the new door delivered and installed or something."

"What's the rush, Josie?"

I stopped my futile weak-limbed efforts at moving furniture and sat down on the loveseat. "I've got places to be, Walker, and I'm not comfortable leaving you here. And anyway, you don't need to be here. Will you please go now or do I need to call one of your vampire enforcers or something?"

"You know, that's the second time you've mentioned enforcers, Josie. What, exactly, do you know about them?"

"Well, that asshole Gregory said that they are the punishment end of your vampire handbook."

"They used to be, but not so much anymore. Do you know what I am, Josie?"

I stood up and walked toward the bed, crossing my arms under my chest. "How the fuck can I know anything about you, Walker? You're so evasive. I don't even know your real name. Just go. Now. I don't want to hear anything else from you."

"Fine." He walked to the door without looking at me, moved the loveseat like it was made out of matchsticks, and disappeared into the humid night.

PART 5 – DEALING WITH VAMPIRE BONDAGE FETISHES

It's not easy to keep sex spicy with a vampire. After living hundreds of years, vampires have just about done it all, perfected it all, and then invented a whole new set of 'all' that you will never experience. Some vampires, however, may have a particular fetish that allows you to keep sex interesting with minimal effort. Some examples include a bondage fetish, foot fetish, latex fetish, stuffed animal…

—Excerpt from *Sex with Vamps - A Guide for Humans*

CHAPTER 18

"So what do you wear on a date with an accountant?" Once again, Alena was on the phone with me trying to help me decide what to wear. After the mess with Gregory and Walker, I took a few weeks to get back into the groove of being dateless, single but still employed as I swore off vampires.

"Now *that* I can help with. Slacks and a blouse. Nothing too worky-but nothing too crazy or sexual. You don't want to intimidate him."

"What the hell are slacks? Is that, like, a pant made out of a special material or something?"

"Josie, slacks are pants, but dressy. Don't be difficult."

"I'm not being difficult, I just don't understand all this special name business. If slacks are pants then why do we need the extra terminology?"

"Anyway, where is Alex taking you?"

"I dunno. We talked on the phone one time and he was so nervous that I don't think he said ten words to me. Seriously, and his voice was super nasal, Alena. Super nasal. I also think I could hear the sound of his handkerchief slopping away his sweat while we spoke. If he brings a handkerchief on this date, I swear I'm just going to walk out."

"Look, I know it's a big letdown to suddenly be dating a human again, but after everything the toothsome duo put you through, I'd think you'd be grateful for a little normalcy. And besides, won't it be nice to go out with a big, strong man and not be huddled up inside your apartment waiting for the boogeyman to kidnap you?"

"Not funny, Alena. Those missing girls really did resemble me and I haven't been huddled, I've simply been…nesting."

She snorted. "Nesting, yeah. And when birds nest, is that when they lick their wounds too?"

"Do birds even have tongues?"

"Josie, do you pay attention to anything going on around you? Look, as enlightening as this conversation is, I think I'd better let you go. Now get dressed, he'll be there soon, won't he?"

I glanced at the clock-five minutes to eight. That gave me five minutes to figure out what slacks were, and since Alex was an accountant, I had a sneaking suspicion that he'd be right on time.

"Yeah, you're right, I gotta go, Alena."

I had just enough time to get dressed and fix my hair before a minivan pulled into my driveway. Why was I not surprised that Alex, the sweaty, nasal accountant, drove a minivan-the least sexy automobile ever created?

I heard a knock and walked to the door. Walker had had the new door delivered and installed the same day he walked out of my house. It had been three weeks and I hadn't heard from him or Gregory. During that time, the smell of cigarettes actually made me a little sad and every now and again

I felt like someone was watching me, but I was convinced that was just another annoying trait of my own egotistical narcissism.

I opened the door and was awash in darkness. I had found my porch light broken when I got home from work the night before and I hadn't had time to replace the bulb...oh, okay. I'd had more than enough time to replace the bulb but I was too lazy. So the porch was dark when I opened the door to greet my sweaty, boring, nervous, and nasal-voiced date. Alena told me that I'd met him at one of her anniversary parties, but for the life of me I could not remember anything about his looks, which was probably a testament to just how forgettable this guy was. I squinted out into the darkness at Alex. "Hi, you must be Alex," I said before the mild-mannered accountant's fist came barreling toward my face. I probably had enough time to move and dodge the fist, but I was in so much shock that I just stood there until the punch connected with my forehead and I was knocked out. While I'm not certain what happened at that point, I'm guessing falling was somehow involved.

CHAPTER 19

I woke up to the persistent dripping of a long-neglected piping system. I was in some sort of warehouse, the kind you see in movies characterized by large, but super-high-up windows covered in chicken wire, with boxes, sheets, and dust everywhere. Beyond the echo of the pipes dripping, I could hear voices that didn't sound exactly happy. The place smelled like old, if old has a smell. Musty, closed up, dusty, and unused.

After determining that I wasn't in immediate danger, I felt courageous enough to figure out how my body was doing so I did a sort of mental countdown of body parts. I was barefoot and my arms were asleep, likely due to the fact that they were pulled tightly behind my back and bound there by a very rough piece of rope that was entwined through the bars on the back of the steel chair I was sitting in. The rope and the knot created a bulge that was biting into my back uncomfortably. My head hurt like I had spent the previous evening with a bottle of Jagermeister and the most sadistic hair stylist to ever apply hair extensions. I was also very hungry.

Next, I did a location assessment. I was in the middle of

the room, smack dab in the center of a puddle of moonlight. I couldn't tell what time it was or what day it was, but the trickle of blood falling from my forehead indicated that either it was relatively soon after I'd been punched or that my captors had been beating me while I was out cold.

I tried to push my fear to the back of my mind and think of some way out of this predicament. I decided to try to hop my chair over to the nearest pile of boxes to see if I could find something sharp to rub my rope-bound wrists on. I straightened my legs and lifted the chair about an inch off the ground. My legs were not bound, so only my wrists were keeping me connected to the chair. I sashayed toward the boxes, hunched over with the chair bouncing off my ass and swinging back and forth like the world's most awkward and useless tail. I got super tired after going only two feet and not reaching any sort of boxes or sharp objects.

I tried to quietly set my chair down on all four legs but instead hit one leg at an angle. It slipped and I fell on my face with my ass-and the chair-pointed up in the air like a sundial and my head bent against the floor at a dangerous angle. At the tremendous noise I made, the angry voices hushed and I heard footsteps coming toward me. I couldn't lift my head but I saw three sets of feet out of the corner of my eye.

"I told you she was going to be trouble," one of the henchmen growled.

Another laughed. "Oh yeah, she's trouble all right. It looks like if we hadn't come along when we did, she'd have asphyxiated herself lying with her head at that angle."

As the area around the edges of my vision darkened and I headed toward sleep, I realized this last henchman was an asshole, but also totally right.

CHAPTER 20

I woke some time later and was once again sitting upright. Although I didn't think it would do any good, I decided to yell for something to drink.

"Um, can I get some water before you kill me?" My fatalistic point of view reverberated off the walls and I realized that I couldn't hear any more henchmen talking. I did hear the clicking of steps coming toward me.

I tossed my head to get my hair out of my eyes so that I could at least see who was holding me here against my will. Imagine my surprise when Gregory, wearing a tuxedo, stepped out of the shadows and into my little puddle of moonlight. He was carrying a bowl that had water sloshing over the side with every step.

"Are you here to save me?" I asked, letting the sad little optimist in me have one last glimmer of hope.

He laughed that thick, rich laugh of his and held the bowl up to my lips with one tanned hand and rested the other hand on the back of my head. He gently tipped the water into my mouth and I gulped at it like a dehydrated baby elephant.

Once I'd had my fill I turned my head slightly to indicate

that I didn't want any more.

"What would you do, Josie, if I didn't recognize what that movement meant? If I shoved this water down your throat until you drowned on it?"

"I guess I would struggle and then drown on it, Gregory. Why the fuck do you ask?"

"Does it make you think more of me that I don't do that, Josie? Because it should. You see, I'm not a cruel man. I don't torture and I'm not needlessly cruel. You will die here, be assured of that, but it will be in the most comfortable way possible."

"Well, I kinda figured you weren't just going to let me go, Gregory. But how kind of you to make it so comfortable for me. Next time you hold some woman against her will, if you're going for comfort, why not try a La-Z-Boy and a television set?"

Gregory laughed, and it no longer warmed me. Now, I was chilled by his mirth and the sparkle in his coal-black eyes. "Once I win this election I won't need to kill any other whores, but I'll definitely make note of your feedback."

"Is that why you're doing this, Gregory? To get the pity vote for your election? The sad murder of a human girl-friend makes the vampire enforcer a vengeance-seeking law upholder?"

"Why, Josie, maybe you are smarter than you look. You see, I got a bad rap last year when the vampire community found one of my supposed kills alive. Now I'm afraid they think I'm not really doing what enforcers are meant to do. Your death will give me a new persona, a reason for being a changed man."

Stalling for time, just a few more minutes to breathe the

sweet taste of life in this dank, moldy warehouse, I asked, "Did you kill the other girls too, Gregory? The ones who sort of looked like me?"

"Naturally. I couldn't just take you and kill you. It had to look like the work of a serial killer-and a vampire, at that. Then everyone would understand how dedicated I would be to enforcing vampire laws and bringing your killer to his justice." As he said all this, Gregory's eyes glazed over and he seemed to be looking into the future, as though it were there just over my left shoulder.

Since my legs were still unattached to the chair, I thought I'd use his distraction to at least kick him in the nuts. I mean, after all, it was the least I could do and, quite literally, the most I could do too. Since I was stuck sitting on a chair, I couldn't exactly work up enough momentum to actually do much damage, but what kind of chick would I be if I did nothing?

I bent my knee and pulled my foot back as much as possible and let my toes point underneath my chair. Then I swiftly lifted it and headed it right toward Gregory's oversized ball sack. Unfortunately, he saw through my movement and grabbed my ankle before it made contact with his balls and used my own momentum against me. He flipped me up so that I landed smartly on my back but still enthroned in the hated chair.

As my blurry gaze tried to focus in on Gregory's laughing face, I saw a tall column of black behind him. I couldn't make out any specific characteristics, but I was certain that I smelled the faint scent of nasty ass cigarettes before I heard Gregory scream like he had been stabbed in the neck with a knife…because he had been stabbed in the neck with a knife, which came all the way through the back of his neck to stick out the front.

"Walker," I mumbled, holding on to consciousness like you might grasp melted butter, "am I dreaming?"

The tall column of black scooted around Gregory's impaled face and rolled my chair over so that he could cut the ropes binding my hands. "Yes, Señorita Ego, it is I, Walker, here to save your life. Now you are really going to owe me." His grumbly, smoke-roughened voice sounded like a choir of angels to my ears as I realized that freedom was within my grasp. Suddenly, he stopped cutting my ropes and I craned my head around to see what was going on. Then he said, "Oh, wait, maybe you want me to leave? What was it you said when you unceremoniously kicked my heart-wrenched soul out of your house? That you didn't want to hear anything else from me?"

"I'm not going to apologize for that, Walker...but I really do want to get out of here and avoid getting killed today, so maybe we can talk this over later, like, at the police station?"

Walker chuckled and resumed cutting my ropes. Once they were completely frayed he unwound them and lifted me up off the floor. I couldn't stand on my own since my body was beaten and bruised and at least one of my head injuries was causing nauseousness and dizzy spells.

I looked down at Gregory's motionless body and asked, "Is he dead?"

"No, he's not dead, but he should be out for a while. He's lost a lot of blood and his body will have thrown him into a stasis of sorts so that it can concentrate its energy on healing. I want to leave him alive so that he can be punished for what he's done. A quick death is too good for him." Walker supported my weight as he led me out the way he had apparently come in.

"You know there are others here helping him, right?" I asked Walker as I did my best to be vigilant for sneaky henchman attacks.

"They're already taken care of, Josie." I stumbled and Walker held me closer to his body. I felt so safe and protected that everything that had happened over the past however many hours finally hit me and I began to shake like someone going through shock. Likely because I was going through shock.

Walker was soothing me and whispering funny little quips in my ear as I saw the open warehouse door and Walker's truck come into view. I tried to speed up, wanting nothing more than to be really safe-like a kid who jumps into bed at night so that the monsters under her bed can't grab her ankles.

Unfortunately, right at that moment, a monster did grab my waist and pulled me out of Walker's grip. Gregory, the monster currently at large, tossed me to the side and I landed in a pile of empty boxes. The knife was gone from his throat, but he had a gaping wound and was still losing blood.

Gregory went for Walker's throat and started choking him. Walker was taller than Gregory, but Gregory's body mass exceeded Walker's and Walker couldn't get out of his grip. Watching as the man who had risked so much to save me was slowly being thwarted, I looked around to see if there were any weapons I could use to put the advantage back in Walker's court. I didn't have much strength, but I tried to push boxes out of the way and eventually I found just what I was looking for, a box cutter, under a pile of broken down boxes.

I grabbed the utilitarian instrument of death and heaved myself up out of the pile. I couldn't let myself think too much about what I was going to do, because bridal shop employees don't generally go all attack on you and cut your throat with box cutters, so this was really disturbing, or it would have been if I let myself consider it.

I was still shaky as I unsteadily made my way to where Gregory and Walker were struggling. My goal was just to cut Gregory's arm so that he would be startled and let go of Walker's throat and then Walker would have the upper hand. Unfortunately, people who are fighting don't just stand still, so while I had aimed for Gregory's arm, they moved as I struck and I ended up nicking Walker's throat above Gregory's fingers.

Even though he was being strangled, Walker took the time to give me a dirty look, which I found completely unnecessary under the circumstances.

As Walker started bleeding, Gregory's hands became slick and it was impossible for Gregory to keep his grip. This, as I planned all along, gave Walker the advantage. As Gregory's hands slipped off Walker's neck, Walker grabbed Gregory's right arm and twisted it around his back. He motioned to me to give him the box cutter, which I did, and he swiftly slit Gregory's throat. As Gregory gurgled and clutched his throat, I tore my shirt off to tie around Walker's neck to stop his bleeding. I moved as if to tie the shirt around his neck myself, but he held up his hands to stop me.

"I think we see how badly your efforts to save me go. I'll just handle the shirt on my own." He saw my concerned and sort of guilty frown, and his hand brushed mine as he took the shirt from me. "Don't worry, Josie, it's just a surface wound."

I looked to where we had left Gregory to make sure he was down, and all I saw was a puddle of blood, the box cutter, and some ashes. Gregory was dead.

PART 6 – HAPPILY EVER AFTER-VAMPIRE STYLE

Dear Vampy,

I think I'm falling in love with a bipolar vampire. I'm willing to hang in there but I need to know-is it ever possible for a human to have a happily ever after with a vampire?

—Josie D. in Florida

Dear Josie,

Only vampires can have a happily ever after-humans just get a happily right now. But don't despair, because even in a relationship with another human, that's really all you can ask for.

—Excerpt from the syndicated *Dear Vampy* column

CHAPTER 21

Since there was no one left alive who was in on Gregory's plan, Walker took me home. On the way, he called a vampire cleanup crew and one of the governors and explained the situation.

Once we reached my house, we both fell into my bed without even cleaning off the blood that was caking us.

"How did you know where I was?" I asked Walker.

"I've been following you for weeks, Josie. Ever since you met Gregory at the party. I was supposed to prevent this from happening to you, but because I didn't know what your accountant date looked like, I left as soon as I saw what I assumed to be him drive up. It was stupid of me, but I just couldn't watch you start a relationship with someone else. And because I had to indulge my own stupid weakness, you almost got killed." He stroked my hair as he recounted the previous evening's events and I could hear his voice shaking.

"Last night? You mean I was in that warehouse for twenty-four hours?"

"Yes, I only realized something had gone wrong when you didn't come home from your date and your friend Alena called your house about thirty times to find out why you weren't there when the accountant actually arrived to pick you up. And on a side note, you might want to tell Alena to get a hobby other than organizing your love life."

"So, you tapped my phone too."

"I had to. I knew Gregory was using you for something, but I couldn't be sure what. Once those girls started going missing, I had a feeling it was part of his overall plan. He's never tried a stunt like this before, so I didn't know to expect it. But I do know that Gregory hates humans, and would never flirt or have a relationship with one unless she was politically influential. That's what made me follow you in the first place."

I scooted back in the bed and sat up, my sudden anger fueling my movement. "So you knew all along that he was using me and you didn't say anything? Was that what all your mood swings were about? You felt guilty letting the little human girl dangle on Gregory's string?"

He sat up and moved closer to me, pulling me into his arms. "No, Josie. To keep you safe I had to watch you and not let you know what I suspected. But as I watched you and got to know you, I began to develop feelings for you. I couldn't let those feelings blind me to my overarching purpose and kept trying to push them back. But when you slept with Gregory, I almost ruined it all with my jealousy. I could have gotten you killed."

"If you started feeling something for me, and didn't want to encourage it, then why ask me on a date? A lame date, by the way, but still, a date."

"I was monitoring you and heard your conversation with Gregory when you called him for the first date. I knew you were going out with him, and I knew that he wouldn't pull anything that quickly, so I thought I could go out with you too. Maybe you might mention our date to him and that would lessen any danger you were in. What I didn't consider was how much that date would affect me."

I wasn't ready yet to address his pronouncements of love or, well, I guess super-deep like would be more accurate, so instead I asked what he was. "So why was it your job to watch over me?"

"I'm an assistant to Governor Harnett. We've been watching Gregory for years trying to get him removed as an enforcer. He was continually taking bribes and relocating the people that he was sent to kill. They'd show up in another country with another identity after decades of supposedly being dead. The last time we found one of them, we decided to make it public so that we could sway opinion against Gregory. We knew he'd strike back but we weren't sure how until I heard that he had flirted with you at his party. When I found that out, I suspected that you were somehow going to work into his plans."

I processed all of this information for a moment, and thought back to all the time Gregory and I had spent together. "Why did he take me to his warehouse when he knew that Governor Harnett knew about it? I mean, the governor specifically asked him about the warehouse while we were at the picnic."

"I can't speak for Gregory, but my guess would be hubris. He was overconfident that no one suspected him of anything."

"So, were all the other girls taken and…um…killed there?" I shuddered as I considered the fact that I'd almost joined those poor girls' ranks.

"I'm so sorry, Josie, but yes, they were. I recovered their bodies after I killed Gregory's guards."

"Oh. Are they or, will they, um, will the families be notified soon? They must be out of their minds with worry. This isn't good news, but it is news and may help them start to heal."

Walker kissed my forehead. "Yes, it's all being taken care of, so don't worry anymore. Why don't you rest?"

I settled in to my bed and Walker's body and I dozed. I'm not sure how long I slept, but it must have been at least twelve hours because it was dusk when I woke. I was in exactly the same position as I had been when I fell asleep and Walker was still there, holding me tightly and stroking my hair.

"You're still here? I thought you'd have some other dame to run off and rescue," I said, by means of good morning.

His hand never paused in stroking my hair, but when he spoke, his voice sounded rough, like it hadn't been used and was overcome with emotion. "I'm right here, where I'll be until you tell me I can't be anymore."

I shivered as I thought about Walker, this strong, sweet, and deeply conflicted man being here with me. Protecting me, comforting me, loving me. "What now, Walker? What happens to us?"

Walker's gravelly voice took on a decidedly sexy tone. "Well, we could take another bath but this time, together. After all, I didn't get to enjoy any of that delicious skin I saw during your last soak. Also, I have lots of fun bath games I'd love to teach you. I've had years and years to develop them."

I laughed. Leave it to a guy to start propositioning me immediately after I've been held hostage, beaten, almost killed, and witnessed a murder. "So much for not sweating the small stuff. Yes, let me call Alena first and let her know I'm okay, then we can take a purely platonic bath together. But then what, Walker?"

"Well, I'll get some time off for a job well done, so I'll probably take a little trip-drive out west maybe. Taste some different air, relax, gear up for the next chore."

"And where does that leave me?"

"Josie, I think you could use a vacation yourself. Have you ever visited the Lone Star State?"

"I have, and I hated it. But then, I wasn't with any cigarette smoking cowboys named Walker."

Walker paused in his ministrations to my hair and his next words came out in an emotion-choked whisper.

"Think you'd like to join me on a sojourn?"

I waited for a minute, not really contemplating the answer I knew I'd give him before he even asked me to join him. "Only if you get your air conditioner in the truck fixed."

Walker sighed and lifted himself over me, so that all his weight was supported by his hands. "It's already done, Josie." His eyes were warm and, it might be jumping the gun, but they looked pretty darned loving as well as relieved. They searched my own as if looking for any sign of hesitance.

"Do I get to learn your real name before we go?"

He laughed. "Let's just save that for another day. I think you've been through enough already."

Not knowing what that was supposed to mean and really, not even caring, I agreed. "Well, then, why don't you kiss me, Walker, and this time, with no rude remarks-just a nice kiss."

And he did.

ABOUT THE AUTHOR

Evelyn Lafont is a freelance writer and author living in Tampa Bay, Florida. Originally from New England, she likes that none of her shoes or body parts freeze during the Florida winter. She is the married mother of two catlike furballs and hates doing housework of any kind.

www.EvelynLafont.Wordpress.com

8728672R0

Made in the USA
Charleston, SC
08 July 2011